KAR

"I've Given Up On Men," Jayla Said.

Storm frowned at her and asked, "And why is that?"

"Because there're too many men out there like you," she replied.

"What is that supposed to mean?"

"You know, the 'love 'em and leave 'em' type," she replied.

He couldn't dispute her words since he was definitely that kind of guy. But still, there was something about hearing it from her that just didn't sit well with him. "Not all men are like me, you know. I'm sure there are some men out there who'd love to get serious with one woman."

Jayla tipped her head back and grinned. "Really? Any recommendations?"

Storm's frown deepened. There was no way he would ever introduce her to any of his friends. Most of them were just like him—genuine players.

"I don't think so," Storm said, and choked down the unfamiliar, sour sensation that burned his stomach at the thought of Jayla in the arms of another man....

Dear Reader,

Welcome to another stellar month of smart, sensual reads. Our bestselling series DYNASTIES: THE DANFORTHS comes to a compelling conclusion with Leanne Banks's *Shocking the Senator* as honest Abe Danforth finally gets his story. Be sure to look for the start of our next family dynasty story when Eileen Wilks launches DYNASTIES: THE ASHTONS next month and brings you all the romance and intrigue you could ever desire…all set in the fabulous Napa Valley.

Award-winning author Jennifer Greene is back this month to conclude THE SCENT OF LAVENDER series with the astounding *Wild in the Moment*. And just as the year brings some things to a close, new excitement blossoms as Alexandra Sellers gives us the next installment of her SONS OF THE DESERT series with *The Ice Maiden's Sheikh*. The always-enjoyable Emilie Rose will wow you with her tale of *Forbidden Passion*—let's just say the book starts with a sexy tryst on a staircase. We'll let you imagine the rest. Brenda Jackson is also back this month with her unforgettable hero Storm Westmoreland, in *Riding the Storm*. (A title that should make you go hmmm.) And rounding things out is up-and-coming author Michelle Celmer's second book, *The Seduction Request*.

I would love to hear what you think about Silhouette Desire, so please feel free to drop me a line c/o Silhouette Books, 233 Broadway, Suite 1001, New York, NY 10279. Let me know what miniseries you are enjoying, your favorite authors and things you would like to see in the future.

With thanks,

Melissa Jeglinski

Melissa Jeglinski
Senior Editor
Silhouette Desire

Please address questions and book requests to:
Silhouette Reader Service
U.S.: 3010 Walden Ave., P.O. Box 1325, Buffalo, NY 14269
Canadian: P.O. Box 609, Fort Erie, Ont. L2A 5X3

RIDING
THE
STORM

BRENDA
JACKSON

Published by Silhouette Books
America's Publisher of Contemporary Romance

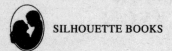 **SILHOUETTE BOOKS**

ISBN 0-373-76625-4

RIDING THE STORM

Books by Brenda Jackson

Silhouette Desire

*Delaney's Desert Sheikh #1473
*A Little Dare #1533
*Thorn's Challenge #1552
Scandal Between the Sheets #1573
*Stone Cold Surrender #1601
*Riding the Storm #1625

*Westmore family titles

BRENDA JACKSON

is a die-"heart" romantic who married her childhood sweetheart and still proudly wears the "going steady" ring he gave her when she was fifteen. Because she's always believed in the power of love, Brenda's stories always have happy endings. In her real-life love story, Brenda and her husband of thirty-two years live in Jacksonville, Florida, and have two sons.

A *USA TODAY* bestselling author, Brenda divides her time between family, writing and working in management at a major insurance company. You may write Brenda at P.O. Box 28267, Jacksonville, Florida 32226, by e-mail at WriterBJackson@aol.com or visit her Web site at www.brendajackson.net.

ACKNOWLEDGEMENTS

To my family and friends.

And to Jayla Ti'ona Hall. This one is for you
when you are old enough to read it.

****

Through wisdom a house is builded,
and by understanding it is established.
—*Proverbs* 24:3

One

"Jayla? What are you doing in New Orleans?"

A gasp of surprise and recognition slipped from Jayla Cole's lips when she quickly turned around. Her gaze immediately connected with that of the tall, dark and dangerously handsome man towering over her as they stood in the lobby of the Sheraton Hotel in the beautiful French Quarter.

There stood Storm Westmoreland. The man had the reputation of being able to talk the panties off any woman who caught his interest. According to what she'd heard, even though Storm sported a clean-cut, all-American-kind-of-a-guy image, he was a master at providing pleasure without promises of forever. The word was that he had the uncanny ability to turn any female's fantasy into reality and had created many memories that were too incredible to forget. Many women considered him the "Perfect Storm."

He was also a man who, for ten years, had avoided her like the plague.

"I arrived in town a couple of days ago to attend the International Organization for Business Communicators convention," she heard herself saying, while trying not to be captivated by the deep darkness of his eyes, the sensual fullness of his lips or the diamond stud he wore in his left ear. And if all that weren't bad enough, there was his skin tone that was the color of semi-sweet chocolate, hair that was cut low and neatly trimmed on his head and the sexiest pair of dimples.

He was dressed in a pair of khakis and a pullover shirt that accentuated his solid frame. His chest was broad and his butt was as tight as she remembered. He always looked good in anything he wore. Her heart accelerated at the memory of her mischievous teenage years when she'd once caught him off guard by boldly brushing up against him. She had thought she'd died and gone to heaven that day. And just like then, Storm was still more than just handsome—he was drop-dead, make-you-want-to-scream, gorgeous.

"What about you?" she decided to ask. "What are you doing in New Orleans?"

"I was here for the International Association of Fire Captains meeting."

She nodded, doing a remarkable job of switching her attention from his strong male features to his words. "I read about your promotion in the newspapers. Dad would have been proud of you, Storm."

"Thanks."

She saw the sadness that immediately appeared in his eyes and understood why. He hadn't gotten over her father's death, either. In fact, the last time she had seen Storm had been at her father's funeral six months ago. He did, however, on occasion call to see how she was doing. Adam Cole had been Storm's first fire captain when he had joined the squad at twenty, over twelve years ago. Her father always thought of Storm as the son he'd never had.

She would never forget the first time her dad had brought him to dinner when she was sixteen. Storm had made quite an impression on her. Not caring that there was a six-year difference in their ages, she'd had a big-time crush on him and would never forget how she had gone out of her way to make him notice her. But no matter how much she'd tried, he never did. And now as she thought back, some of her tactics had been rather outrageous as well as embarrassing. Thank goodness Storm had taken all of her antics in stride and had rebuffed her advances in a genteel way. Now, at twenty-six, she was ten years older and wiser, and she could admit something she had refused to admit then. The man was not her type and was totally out of her league.

"So, how long will you be in The Big Easy?" he asked, breaking once again into her thoughts.

"I'll be here for the rest of the week. The conference ended today, but I've made plans to stick around until Sunday to take in the sights. I haven't been to New Orleans in over five years."

He smiled and it was a smile that made her insides feel jittery. "I was here a couple of years ago and totally enjoyed myself," he said.

She couldn't help wondering if he'd come with a woman or if he'd made the trip with his brothers. Everyone who'd lived in the Atlanta area for an extended period of time was familiar with the Westmoreland brothers—

Dare, Thorn, Stone, Chase and Storm. Their only sister, Delaney, who was the youngest of the siblings, had made news a couple years ago when she married a desert sheikh from the Middle East.

Dare Westmoreland was a sheriff in a suburb of Atlanta called College Park; Thorn was well-known nationally for the motorcycles he raced and built; Stone, who wrote under the pen name of Rock Mason, was a national bestselling author of action-thriller novels and Chase, Storm's fraternal twin, owned a soul-food restaurant in downtown Atlanta.

"So how long do you plan on staying?" she asked.

"My meeting ended today. Like you, I plan on staying until Sunday to take in the sights and to eat my fill of Cajun food."

His words had sounded so husky and sexy she could actually feel her throat tighten.

"How would you like to join me for dinner?"

Jayla blinked, not sure she had heard him correctly. "Excuse me?"

He gave her what had to be his Perfect Storm sexy smile. "I said how would you like to join me for dinner? I haven't seen you since Adam's funeral, and although we've talked briefly on the phone a couple of times since then, I'd love to sit and chat with you to see how you've been doing."

A part of her flinched inside. His words reminded her of the promise he had made to her father before he'd died—that if she ever needed anything, he would be there for her. She didn't relish the thought of another domineering man in her life, especially one who reminded her so much of her father. The reason Storm and Adam Cole had gotten along so well was because they'd thought a lot alike.

"Thanks for the offer, but I've already made plans for later," she said, lying through her teeth.

It seemed that turning down his offer didn't faze him one bit. He merely shrugged his shoulders before checking his watch. "All right, but if you change your mind give me a call. I'm in Room 536."

"Thanks, I'll do that."

He looked at her and smiled. "It was good seeing you again, Jayla, and if you ever need anything don't hesitate to call me."

If he really believed she would call him, then he didn't know her at all, Jayla quickly thought. Her father may have thought of Storm as a son, but she'd never considered him a brother. In her mind, he had been the guy who could make her all hot and bothered; the guy who was the perfect figment of a teenage girl's imagination. He had been real, bigger than life and for two solid years before leaving Atlanta to attend college, he had been the one person who had consumed all of her thoughts.

When she returned home four years ago, she had still found him totally irresistible, but it didn't take long to realize that he still wouldn't give her the time of day.

"And it was good seeing you again, too, Storm. Just in case we don't run into each other again while we're here, I hope you have a safe trip back to Atlanta," she said, hoping she sounded a lot more excited than she actually felt.

"And I ditto that for you," he said. He surprised her when he grasped her fingers and held them firmly. She'd shivered for a second before she could stop herself. His touch had been like a shock. She couldn't help noticing how strong his hand was, and his gaze was deep and intent. She remembered another time their gazes had connected in such a way. It had been last year, when the men at the fire station had given her father a surprise birthday party. She distinctively remembered Storm standing across the room talking to someone and then suddenly turning, locking his gaze with hers as if he were actually seeing her for the first time. The episode had been brief, but earth-tilting for her nonetheless.

"Your father was a very special man, Jayla, and he meant a lot to me," he said softly before releasing his grip and taking a step back.

She nodded, putting how intense Storm's nearness made her feel to the back of her mind while holding back the tears that always flooded her eyes whenever she thought of losing her father to pancreatic cancer. He had died within three months of the condition being diagnosed.

Although while growing up she had thought he was too authoritative at times, he had been a loving father. "And you meant a lot to him, as well, Storm," she said, through the tightness in her throat. "You were the son he never had."

She watched him inhale deeply and knew that her words had touched him.

"Promise that if you ever need anything that you'll call me."

She sighed, knowing she would have to lie to him for a second time that day. "I will, Storm."

Evidently satisfied with her answer, he turned and walked away. She watched, transfixed, trying to ignore how the solid muscles of his body yielded beneath the material of his shirt and pants. The last thought that came into her mind before he stepped into the elevator was that he certainly did have a great-looking butt.

* * *

When the elevator door swooshed shut, Storm leaned back against the back wall to get his bearings. Seeing Jayla Cole had had one hell of an effect on him. She had been cute and adorable at sixteen, but over the years she had grown into the most breathtaking creature he'd ever set his eyes on.

"Jayla." He said her name softly, drawing out the sound with a deep, husky sigh. He would never forget the time Adam had invited him to dinner to celebrate Jayla's return to Atlanta from college. It was supposed to have been a very simple and quiet affair and had ended up being far from it. He had walked into the house and felt as if someone had punched him in the stomach. The air had miraculously been sucked from his lungs.

Jayla had become a woman, a very beautiful and desirable woman, and the only thing that had kept him from adding her to his To Do list was the deep respect he'd had for her father. But that hadn't kept her from occasionally creeping into his dreams at night or from being the lone person on his Would Definitely Do If I Could list.

He sighed deeply. She had the most luscious pair of whiskey-colored eyes he'd ever seen, medium brown hair that shimmered with strands of golden highlights and skin the color of creamy cocoa. He thought the entire combination went far beyond classic beauty. And he hadn't been able to ignore just how good her body looked in the shorts and tank top she'd been wearing and how great she'd smelled. He hadn't recognized the fragrance and he'd thought he knew them all.

She had actually trembled when he'd reached out and touched her hand. He'd felt it and her responsiveness to his touch had given his body a jump-start. It had taken everything within him to pretend he wasn't affected by her. Since he was thirty-two, he calculated that Jayla was now twenty-six. She was now a full-grown woman. All woman. But still there was something about her that radiated an innocence he'd seldom found in women her age. It was her innocence that confused him most. He was an ace at figuring out women, but there was something about her that left him a bit mystified and he couldn't shake the feeling. But one thing he was certain about—as far as he was concerned, Jayla was still off-limits.

Maybe it had been a blessing that she'd turned down his invitation to dinner. The last thing he needed was to share a meal with her. In fact, spending any amount of time with her would only be asking for trouble, considering his attraction to her. He released a moan, a deep throaty sound, and realized that the only thing that had changed with the situation was that Adam was no longer alive to serve as a buffer and a constant reminder of the one woman he could not have.

"Damn."

Just thinking about Jayla sent a jolt of desire straight from the bottom of his feet to the top of his head, leaving an aching throb in his midsection. Storm rubbed a hand down his face. Nothing had changed. The woman was still too much temptation. She'd been a handful while growing up; Adam had been faced with the challenge of raising his daughter alone after his wife died, when Jayla was ten.

Adam had been a strict father, too strict at times, Storm thought, but he'd wanted to keep his daughter safe and not allow her to get into the kind of trouble other teenagers were getting into. But Adam had also been a loving and caring father and had always placed Jayla first in his life. Storm had always admired the man for that.

Storm's thoughts went back to Jayla and the outfit she was wearing. It hadn't been blatantly sexy, but it had definitely captured his interest. But that was as far as he would allow it to go, he thought with a resigned sigh. Jayla was definitely not his type.

He enjoyed his freedom-loving ways too much and no matter what anyone thought, he knew the main reason he lived a stress-free life was because of his active sex life. In his line of business, you needed an outlet when things got too overbearing. And as long as he was responsible and made sure all his encounters didn't involve any health risks, he would continue to engage in the pleasures of sex.

Okay, so he would admit that he was a man with commitment issues, thanks to Nicole Brown. So what if it had been fifteen years, there were some things a man didn't forget and rejection was one of them.

He and Nicole had dated during his senior year in high school and had even talked about getting married when he finished college. He would never forget the night he had told Nicole that his future plans had changed. He decided that, unlike his brothers, he didn't want to go to college. Instead, he wanted to stay in Atlanta and attend the Firefighters Academy. Nicole hadn't wasted any time in telling him what she thought about his plans. A man without a college education could not provide adequately for a family, she'd told him, and had broken up with him that same night.

He had loved her and her rejection had hurt. It had also taught him a very valuable lesson. Keep your heart to yourself. You could have sex for sex's sake, but love and marriage would never be part of the mix. So what if his uncle Corey, who had pledged to remain a bachelor for life, as well as his older brothers Dare, Thorn and Stone, had all gotten married in less than a year? That didn't mean he or his twin Chase would follow in their footsteps.

His thoughts shifted back to Nicole. He had seen her at a class reunion a few years back and had been grateful things had ended between them when they had. After three marriages, she was still looking for what she considered the perfect man with a good education and plenty of money. She had been surprised to learn that because firefighters made it a point to constantly study to improve their job performance and prepare for promotional exams, he had eventually gone to college, taking classes at night to earn a bachelor's degree in fire science and later a master's degree in public administration.

His thoughts left Nicole and went back to Jayla. He remembered when she had left Atlanta to attend a college in the north. Adam had wanted her to stay closer to home, but had relented and let her go. Adam would keep him updated on how well she was doing in school. He'd always been the proud father and when she had graduated at the top of her class, Adam had taken all the men in his squad out to celebrate. That had been four years ago....

The chiming of the elevator interrupted his reverie. The elevator opened on his floor and Storm stepped out. He had reached the conclusion that, incredible-looking or not, the last woman he would want to become involved with was Jayla Cole. But once again he thought about how she looked downstairs in the lobby. Incredible. Simply incredible...

The next morning, Jayla leaned back in her chair at the hotel restaurant, sipped her orange juice and smiled brightly. The call she had received before leaving her hotel room had made her very happy. Ecstatic was more like it.

The fertility clinic had called to let her know that everything had checked out and they had found a sperm donor whose profile met all of her requirements. There was a possibility they could schedule the procedure in less than a month.

She felt downright giddy at the thought of having a child. Her mother had died when she was ten, and her father's recent death had left her suffering with occasional bouts of loneliness. She had been an only child; she never had a sibling to share that special closeness with and now more than ever she wanted a child to love and to add special meaning to her life.

At first, she had looked at the pool of guys she had dated over the past couple of years, but for the most part they left a lot to be desired—they'd been either too overbearing or too overboring. So she'd decided to try a fertility clinic. After doing a load of research she had moved ahead with the preliminary paper work. Now in less than two months, she would take the first steps in becoming a new mother. A huge smile touched her lips. She couldn't wait to hold her baby in her arms. Her precious little one would have chocolate-colored skin, dark eyes, curvy full lips, cute dimples and...

"Good morning, Jayla. You seem to be in a rather good mood this morning."

Jayla looked up and met Storm's gaze. Although she had decided to avoid him for the remainder of her time in New Orleans, she wasn't upset that they had run into each other again so soon. She was too elated with life to let anything or anyone dampen her spirits today.

"I *am* in a good mood, Storm. I just received some wonderful news," she said smiling brightly. She saw the curiosity in his eyes, but knew he was too well-mannered to ask her for any details. And she had no intention of sharing her plans with him. Her decision to venture into single parenthood was personal and private. She hadn't shared it with anyone, not even Lisa, her best friend from work.

"Mind if I join you?"

Her smile widened. "Yes, have a seat."

She watched as he sat down and noticed his outfit complemented his physique just as it had the day before. He definitely looked good in a pair of cutoff jeans and a T-shirt that said Firefighters Are Hot.

"So what are you having this morning?" he asked, glancing over at her plate.

"Buffet. And everything is delicious."

He nodded. "Umm, I think I'll try it myself."

No sooner had he said the last word, a waiter appeared and Storm informed the man that he would be having the buffet. "I'll be back in a minute," he said standing.

Jayla watched as he made his way across the room to where the buffet was set up. She couldn't help but watch him. She knew there was no way she could feel guilty about being drawn to him, since she had always been attracted to him. And at least she wasn't the only one, she thought, glancing around and seeing that a number of admiring women had turned to check him out. However, it appeared he was more interested in filling his plate than in all the attention he was getting.

Jayla blinked when she suddenly realized something. Storm's features were identical to those she had requested when she'd filled out the questionnaire for the fertility clinic. If the clinic filled her request to the letter, the donor whose sperm she would receive would favor Storm and her baby would almost be his clone.

She shook her head, not believing what she'd subconsciously done. When she blinked again, she noticed that Storm had caught her staring at him, lifted his brow in question and then stared back at her.

Jayla's heart thudded in her chest as she watched as he crossed the room back to her with a plate filled to capacity. "Okay, what'd I do?" he asked sitting down. "You were staring at me like I'd suddenly grown an extra nose or something."

This time, Jayla had to force herself to smile. "No, you're fine. I just couldn't help but notice how much food you were piling on your plate," she said instead of telling him the real reason she'd been staring.

He chuckled. "Hey, I'm a growing boy. All my brothers and I eat like this."

Jayla took another sip of orange juice. She had met his brothers a while back and remembered all four of them being in excellent shape. If they routinely ate that much food, they must also work out…a lot. "Your parents must have had one heck of a grocery bill."

"They did, and while we were growing up my mom didn't work outside of the home, so it was up to my dad to bring home the bacon. And not once did he complain about the amount of money being spent on food. That's the way I want it in my household *if* I ever marry."

Jayla lifted a brow after taking another sip of orange juice. "What?"

"I don't want my wife to work outside of the home."

Jayla gazed at him as she set down her glass. She had

heard that very thing from several people who knew him. It was no secret that when Storm Westmoreland married, he would select a domestic diva.

"I have deep admiration and respect for any woman who works inside the home raising her family," she said truthfully.

His features showed signs of surprise. "You do?"

"Yes, raising a family is a full-time job."

He leaned back in his chair and studied her for a moment before asking, "So you would do it? You would be a stay-at-home-mom?"

"No."

He sat up straight. "But you just said that you—"

"Admired women who did it, but that doesn't necessarily mean that I would do it. I believe I can handle a career and motherhood and chose to have both."

"It won't be easy."

Jayla chuckled as she pushed aside her plate. "Nothing about being a parent is easy, Storm, whether you work in the home or outside the home. The most important thing is making sure the child is loved and well taken care of. Now if you will excuse me, I think I will try some of that fruit."

Storm watched as she stood and crossed the room. Wasn't it just yesterday that he had decided to stay away from her because she was too much of a temptation? When he had walked into the restaurant, he had sensed her presence even before he had actually seen her. Then he had glanced around and his gaze had locked in on her sitting alone at a table, drinking her orange juice with a huge smile on her face, completely oblivious to anyone and anything around her. Even now, he couldn't help but wonder what had put her in such a good mood.

He took a sip of his coffee, thinking she evidently didn't want him to know since she hadn't shared whatever it was with him. Electricity shot through him as he continued to watch as she put an assortment of fruit into a bowl. He liked the outfit she was wearing, a fuchsia sundress with spaghetti straps and a pair of flat sandals on her feet. She had gorgeous legs, and her hair flowed around her shoulders, emphasizing her beauty from every angle. She looked the very image of sexiness and at the same time she looked comfortable and ready for the New Orleans heat that was normal for a September day.

"The food in this place is good," she said returning to the table and digging into the different fruits she had brought back with her.

He lifted his dark head and his stomach tightened as he watched her slip a slice of pineapple into her mouth and relish it as if it were the best thing she'd ever eaten. She chewed very slowly while his gaze stayed glued to her mouth, finding the entire ordeal fascinating as well as arousing.

"So, what are you plans for today?"

Her question reeled him back in. He set his fork down and leaned back in his chair. He met her gaze, or at least tried to, without lowering it to her mouth again. "Take in the sights. I checked with the person at the concierge's desk and he suggested I do the Gray Line bus tour."

Jayla smiled brightly. "Hey, he gave me the same suggestion. Do you want to do it together?"

Innocent as it was, he wished she hadn't invited him to join her sightseeing expedition in precisely those words. *Do it together.* A totally different scenario than what she was proposing popped into his head and he was having a hard time getting it out of there. "You sure you don't mind the company?" he asked searching her face. Although he got very few, he recognized a brush-off when he got one and yesterday, after asking her to dinner, she had definitely given him the brush-off.

"No, I'd love the company."

He wondered what had changed her mood. Evidently the news she'd received had turned the snotty Jayla of last night into Miss Congeniality this morning.

"So what do you say, Mr. Fireman? Shall we hit the streets?"

Hitting the sheets was more to his liking, but he immediately reminded himself just who she was and that she was still off-limits. "Sure. I think it would be fun." *As long as we keep things simple,* he wanted to add but didn't.

She chuckled, a low, sexy sound, as she leaned forward. "And that's what I need, Storm, some honest-to-goodness fun."

He looked at her for a moment, then suddenly understood. The past six months had to have been hard. She and her father had been extremely close, so no doubt the loneliness was finally getting to her.

A jolt of protectiveness shot through him. Hadn't he promised Adam that he would look after her? Besides, if anyone could show her how to have fun, he could. Because of his attraction to her, over the years he had basically tried to avoid her. Now it seemed that doing so had robbed him of the chance to get to know her better. Maybe it was time that he took the first step to rectify the situation so that a relationship, one of friendship only, could develop between them.

Having fun with a woman without the involvement of

sex would be something new for him, but he was willing to try it. Since there was no way the two of them could ever be serious, he saw nothing wrong with letting his guard down and having a good time. "Then I will give you a day of fun, Jayla Cole," he said and meaning every word.

A smile touched the corners of his mouth. "And who knows? You just might surprise yourself and have so much fun, you may not ever want to get serious again."

Two

A rush of excitement shot through Jayla's bloodstream when the bus made another stop on its tour. This time to board the *Steamboat Natchez* for a cruise along the Mississippi River. So far, she and Storm had taken a carriage ride through the French Quarter, a tour of the swamps and visited a number of magnificently restored mansions and courtyards.

The *Natchez* was a beautiful replica of the steamboats that once cruised the Mississippi. Jayla stood at the railing appreciating the majestic beauty of the river and all the historical landmarks as they navigated its muddy waters. She was very much aware of the man standing beside her. During the boat ride, Storm had kept her amused by telling her interesting tidbits of information about riverboats.

As he talked, she tipped her head and studied him, letting eyes that were hidden behind the dark lenses of her sunglasses roam over him. She enjoyed looking at him as much as she enjoyed listening to him. Soft jazz was flowing through several speakers that were located on the lower deck and the sound of the boat gliding through the water had a relaxing effect on Jayla.

When Storm fell silent for a few moments, Jayla figured she needed to say something to assure him that he had her full attention, which he definitely did. "How do you know so much about riverboats?" she asked, genuinely curious. She watched his lips curve into a smile and a flutter went through her stomach.

"Mainly because of my cousin Ian," he replied as he absently flicked a strand of hair away from her face. "A few years ago, he and some investor friends of his decided to buy a beauty of a riverboat. It's over four hundred feet long and ninety feet high, and equipped with enough staterooms to hold over four hundred passengers."

"Wow! Where does it go?"

Storm leaned back against the rail and placed his hands in the pockets of his shorts. "Ian's riverboat, *The Delta Princess,* departs from Memphis on ten-day excursions along the Mississippi with stops in New Orleans, Baton Rouge, Vicksburg and Natchez. His crew provides first-class service and the food he serves on board is excellent. In the beginning, business was slow, but now he has reservations booked well over a year in advance. It didn't take him long to figure out what would be a drawing card."

Jayla lifted a brow. "What?"

"Gambling. You'd be surprised how many people have money they figure is worth losing if there's a chance that they might win more."

Jayla could believe that. A couple of years ago, she and

Lisa had taken a trip to Vegas and had seen first hand just how hungry to win some people were.

When there was another lull in the conversation, she turned away from him to look out over the river once more. It was peaceful, nothing like the tempest that was raging through her at the moment. Storm had kept his word. She'd had more fun today with him than she'd had in a long time. He possessed a fun-loving attitude that had spilled over to her. There were times when he had shared a joke with her that had her laughing so hard she actually thought something inside her body would break. It had felt good to laugh, and she was glad she'd been able to laugh with him.

She tried to think of the last time she had laughed with a man and recalled that it had been with her father. Even during his final days, when she'd known that pain had racked his body, he'd been able to tell a good joke every now and then. She heaved a small sigh. She missed her father so much. Because he had kept such a tight rein on her, she had been a rebellious teen while growing up. It was only when she'd returned from college that she had allowed herself to form that special father-daughter relationship with him.

After his death, at the encouragement of the officials at the hospice facility, she had gone through grief counseling and was glad she had. It had helped to let go and move on. One of the biggest decisions she'd been forced to make was whether to sell her parents' home and move into a smaller place. After much soul-searching, she had made a decision to move. She loved her new home and knew once she had her baby, it wouldn't be as lonely as it was now. She was getting excited again just thinking about it.

"So what are your plans for later?"

Storm's question invaded her thoughts and she tipped her head to look over at him. "My plans for later?"

"Yes. Yesterday, I invited you to join me for dinner and you turned me down, saying you'd already made plans. Today, I'm hoping to ask early enough so that I'll catch you before you make other arrangements."

Jayla sighed. She knew her mind needed a reality check, but she wasn't ready to give it one. Spending the day with Storm had been nice; it had been fun and definitely what she'd needed. But she didn't need to spend her evening with him as well. The only thing the two of them had in common was the fact they both loved and respected her father. That would be the common link they would always share. But spending more time with Storm would only reawaken all those old feelings of attraction she had always had for him.

She took off her sunglasses, met his gaze directly and immediately wished she hadn't. His eyes were dark, so dark you could barely see the pupils. The jolt that passed through her was so startling she had to remind herself to breathe.

"I was wondering when you were going to stop hiding behind these," he said, taking the sunglasses out of her hand when she was about to put them back on. He gave her a cocky smile. "But I didn't mind you checking me out."

Jayla couldn't hide the blush that darkened her cheeks. Nor could she resist easing her lips into a smile. So he'd known she had been looking him over. "I guess it probably gets rather annoying to you after a while, doesn't it?"

He arched a brow. "What?"

"Women constantly checking you out."

He smiled again. "Not really. Usually I beat them to the

punch and check them out, so by the time they decide they're interested, I know whether or not I am."

A grin tilted the corners of Jayla's lips. "Umm, such arrogance." She took her sunglasses from him and put them back on, preferring her shield.

"Instead of arrogance, I see it as not wasting time," he said simply. "I guess you can say I weed out those who won't make the cut."

Jayla sighed deeply and struggled with good judgment as to whether to ask her next question. Although she may have struggled with it, curiosity got the best of her. She couldn't help but ask, "So, did I make the cut?"

For a moment, she thought he would not answer. Then he leaned forward, pulled off her sunglasses and met her gaze. "With flying colors, Jayla Cole. I'm a hot-blooded man and would be telling a lie if I said I didn't find you attractive. But then, on the other hand, I have to respect who you'll always be to me."

"Adam's daughter?"

"Yes."

Jayla had to resist grinding her teeth in frustration. She doubted he realized that he'd hit a sore spot with her. Not because she was Adam Cole's daughter, but because being her father's daughter had been the reason Storm had always kept his distance from her. A part of her had gotten over his rejection years ago, but still, it downright infuriated her that he had labeled her as "hands off" because of his relationship with her father.

She watched as he pointedly checked his watch, as if to signal their topic of conversation was now over. "You never did say whether or not you had plans for later."

Jayla almost reached out to snatch her sunglasses from

his hand again, then changed her mind. Instead, she decided to have a little fun with him. She stepped close to him, reached out and took hold of the front of his shirt. "Why, Storm? What do you have in mind for later?" she asked, in a very suggestive tone of voice.

She watched as he studied her features with a well-practiced eye before he said, "Dinner."

She pressed a little closer to him. "Dinner? That's it?"

He glanced around. There were only a handful of people about. Most had gone up on deck to listen to the live jazz band that was performing. His gaze returned to hers. "Yes, that's it. Unless…"

She lifted a brow. "Unless what?" she asked, then watched as his mouth curved into a smile. A very sexy smile.

"Unless you want me to toss you into the river to cool off."

Jayla blinked. His smile was gone and the dark eyes staring at her were serious. She stared back, willing him to get the message she was sending with her eyes. His words had ticked her off. "Do you think I need to cool off, Storm?"

The smile that returned to his lips came slow, but it came nonetheless. "I think you need to behave, brat," he said, playfully tweaking her nose.

She frowned. Those were the same words he had spoken to her ten years earlier when she had made that pass at him. She knew he'd been as right then as he was now, but, dammit, it really annoyed her that he was still using her father as an excuse to keep her at arm's length. A part of her knew it was ludicrous for her to be upset, especially when she should probably be grateful, considering his "wham, bam, thank you, ma'am" reputation.

His Don Juan exploits were legendary. Even so, a part

of her hated his refusal to acknowledge she was not a child any longer. She was a full-grown woman and it was up to her to decide whom she was interested in and whom she wanted a relationship with. After all, pretty soon she would be a woman with the responsibility of raising a child alone.

"So, what about dinner, Jayla?"

Time seemed to stop as Jayla considered her options. On the one hand, having dinner with him was a really bad idea. She sure didn't need someone like Storm in her life, especially with her plans with the fertility clinic and her future as a single mom a definite go. That's what the rational part of her brain was trying to get through to her. On the other hand, there was that irrational part, the one that resented him for being all knowing and too damn caring. That part of her head said that one little dinner would do no harm. She knew she should leave well enough alone, but part of her just couldn't.

She met his gaze. "I'll think about it." And without saying anything else, she took her sunglasses from his hand and walked away.

Storm shook his head as he watched Jayla stroll across the deck. She'd had a lot of nerve asking if she made the cut, as if she hadn't felt the sparks that had flown between them yesterday as well as most of the morning. Fortunately for him, it was an attraction that he could control. But he had to admit that when she had pretended to come on to him a few moments ago, he had almost broken out in a sweat.

He remembered her teen years. During that time Adam described her as headstrong, free-spirited and an independent thinker. It seemed not much about her had changed.

Storm watched as she moved around the tables that were filled to capacity with an assortment of food and knew he had to rethink his relationship with her. A lot about Jayla *had* changed and he was looking his fill, taking all those changes in at that very moment.

He couldn't remember the last time any woman had gotten his attention the way Jayla had. She didn't know how close she'd come to getting a kiss from him when she had molded her body to his. His gaze had latched on to her lips. They had looked so soft that he'd wanted to find out for himself just how soft and kissable they were.

He sighed. Her ploy had been no more than teasing, but his body was still reeling from the effects. However, no matter what, he had to keep her best interests at heart, even if she didn't know what her best interests were and even if it killed him.

Why couldn't he keep his eyes off her? Hadn't he decided she was off-limits? He glanced away and tried to focus on the beauty of the river as the riverboat continued to move through it. It was a beautiful September day and he had to admit he was enjoying Jayla's company. She had a knack for making him want to see her smile, hear her laugh; he could honestly say he had relished his time with her more than he had any woman in a long time.

He wondered if she was romantically involved with anyone. He recalled Adam mentioning once that he felt she was too nitpicky when it came to men and that she would never meet the "perfect man" that met her satisfaction. That conversation has taken place years ago and Storm couldn't help wondering if her attitude had changed. Had she found someone? Something or someone had definitely had her smiling when he'd first seen her at breakfast that morning. All she'd said was that she had just received some wonderful news, news she hadn't bothered sharing with him. Did the news have anything to do with a lover?

"Storm, don't you want something to eat?"

The sound of her voice grabbed his attention and he glanced back over to her, met her gaze and had to swallow. The hue of her eyes seemed to pull him to her. And he didn't want to think about her mouth, a mouth that now contained a pulse-stopping smile. It seems the feathers he had ruffled earlier were now all smoothed. When he didn't answer quickly enough, she quirked a brow and asked, "Well, do you?"

He fought the urge to tell her yes, that he was hungry, but what he wanted had nothing to do with food. Instead of saying anything, he strolled over to join her at the table and took the plate she offered him. "Yes. Thanks."

"You're welcome. You might want to try these, they're good," she said popping a Cajun cheese ball into her mouth.

Storm's breath hitched. He watched her chew, seeing her mouth barely moving. He quickly decided it wouldn't be that way if they were to kiss. He definitely intended to get a lot of movement out of that mouth. He continued to stare at her mouth for a moment and then sighed. Thinking about kissing her was not the way to go. He needed to concentrate on sharing a platonic relationship with her and nothing more,

"If you eat enough of these, there might not have to be a *later*."

Her words reclaimed his attention. "Excuse me?"

She smiled. "I said if you eat enough of these you might be able to forgo dinner later. They're so delicious."

His first instinct was to tell her that to him, food was like sex—he rarely got enough of it. But he decided telling her that wasn't a good idea. After they had both filled their plates, they walked up the steps to the upper deck where tables and chairs were located.

His attention shifted to claiming a table close to the rails so they could continue to enjoy the view of the river while they ate. When they were both seated, he turned his attention back to her. Her hair was blowing in the midday breeze and he stared at the magnitude of her beauty once again. While his attention was on her, her attention was on her food. Most people who came to New Orleans appreciated its culinary excellence and he could tell by the way she was enjoying her bowl of seafood gumbo that she was enjoying the cuisine, too.

Instead of concentrating on his food, Storm was becoming obsessed with a question. When he realized that he wasn't going to be able to eat before he got an answer, he decided to come out and ask her the one question that was gnawing at him.

"So, are you seeing anyone seriously, Jayla?"

He watched her lift her head and met his gaze. She smiled. "No, I've given up on men."

Storm frowned. Her answer was not what he had expected. "Why?"

She leaned back in her chair. "Because there're too many out there like you."

He leaned forward, lifting a dark brow. "And how am I?"

"The 'love them and leave them' type."

He couldn't dispute her words since he was definitely that. But still, there was something about hearing it from her that just didn't sit well with him. "Not all men are like me. I'm sure there are some who'd love to get serious with one woman and make a commitment."

She tipped her head back and grinned. "Really? Any recommendations?"

His frown deepened. There was no way he would ever introduce her to any of his friends. Most of them were players, just like him, and his only unmarried brother was too involved with his restaurant to indulge in a serious relationship. His thoughts then fell on his six male cousins, eight now if you counted the most recent additions to the Westmoreland family—the two sons his uncle Corey hadn't known about until recently. But still, he wouldn't dare introduce her to any of them either. If she was off-limits to him, then she was off-limits to them, as well.

"No," he decided to answer. "There aren't any I can recommend. Where have you been looking?"

She chuckled as she went back to her gumbo. "Nowhere lately, since I'm no longer interested. But when I was interested I tried everywhere—bars, clubs, blind dates and I even used the Internet."

Storm's mouth fell open. "The Internet?"

She smiled at the look of shock on his face. "Yes, the Internet and I have to admit that I thought I had gotten a very promising prospect…until I actually met him. He was at least fifteen years older than the picture he had on the Web site made him seem and instead of having two hands, it seemed he had a dozen. I had to almost deck him a few times for trying to touch me in places that he shouldn't."

Storm's hands trembled in anger at the thought that she had done something so foolish as to place herself in that situation. No wonder Adam had asked him to look out for her. Now he regretted that he hadn't done a better job at it. He could imagine any man wanting to touch her body, since it was so tempting, but wanting to touch her and actually doing it were two different things. "Don't ever date anyone off the Internet again," he all but snarled.

Jayla grinned. "Why, Storm, if I didn't know better, I'd think you were jealous," she said playfully.

Storm wasn't in a playful mood. "Jealous, hell. I'm just trying to look out for you. What if that guy would have placed you in a situation you couldn't get out of?"

Jayla raised her gaze upward. "Jeez, give me the benefit of having common sense, Storm. We met in a public place and—"

"He was groping you in a public place?"

She took a sip of her drink and then said, "We were dancing."

Storm took a deep, calming breath as he tried reeling in his anger. "I hope you learned a lesson."

"I did, and there's another reason I've given up on men."

He raised a brow. "Yeah, what's that?"

Her eyes turned serious. "Most are too controlling, which is something I definitely don't need after having Adam Cole for a father. I didn't start dating until I was seventeen, and I wasn't allowed to do sleepovers at my friends' homes."

Storm frowned. "There was nothing wrong with your father wanting to protect you, Jayla. I'm sure it wasn't easy for a single man to raise a daughter, especially one as spirited and defiant as I'd heard you could be at times."

Jayla shrugged. "Well, whatever. You wanted to know the reasons I'd given up on men and I've just told you why I don't date anymore. I figured what the hell, why bother. Men are too much trouble."

The eyes that were gazing up at him were big, round, sexy and serious. He shook his head. To tell the truth, he'd often thought women were too much trouble, too, but at no time had he considered giving them up. "I don't think you should write men off completely."

The jazz band that had taken a break earlier started back up again and conversation between him and Jayla ended. While she became absorbed in the musicians, he sat back and studied her for a long time. Being concerned about his late mentor's bratty daughter meant he was a good friend and not a jealous suitor as she'd claimed. He never cared enough about a woman to become jealous and Jayla Cole was no exception…or was she?

Jayla sipped her drink and half listened to the musicians who were performing a very jazzy tune. Of course she had recognized Storm's concern as a protective gesture but still, she couldn't resist ribbing him about being jealous.

He was so easy to tease. Charming, gorgeous and sexy as sin. But what she'd told him had been the truth. She had basically written men off. That's why she had decided to use the fertility clinic instead of a live donor.

She had made up in her mind that marriage wasn't for her. She enjoyed her independence too much to have to answer to anyone, and men had a way looking at their wives as possessions instead of partners, a lover for life, his other half and his soul mate. Her time and concentration would be focused on having her baby and raising it. Then later, if she did meet someone who met her qualifications, he would have to take the total package—her and her child.

She glanced over at Storm and saw his full attention was focused on the musicians. There was a dark scowl on his face and she wondered if he was still thinking about her and the Internet man.

Running into him in New Orleans was definitely an un-expected treat. She decided to enjoy the opportunity while it lasted. So far, their day together had been so much fun…at least for half the time. The other half of their time together she'd been too busy fighting her attraction to him to really enjoy herself. He was no different from the other men she had dated—possibly even worse—but that didn't stop that slow sizzle from moving through her body when-ever he looked at her.

A part of her couldn't help but wonder if all the things she'd heard about him were fact or myth.

"The riverboat has returned to dock, Jayla."

His words, spoken low and in a husky tone, intruded into her thoughts. She glanced around and saw that the river-boat had returned to the Toulouse Street Wharf. "We re-turned sooner than I thought we would," she said, forcing down the lump of disappointment that suddenly appeared in her throat.

"We've been cruising the Mississippi for over three hours," he said, returning the irrepressible smile that had recently vanished from his lips. "Don't you think it's time we got back?"

She shrugged, wondering if he'd gotten bored with her already. Without saying a word, she stood and began gath-ering up the debris from their meal. He reached out and stopped her. She looked up and met his gaze.

"I'm not one of those men who expects a woman to clean up after him."

She opened her mouth to speak, but the words wouldn't come out. His hand was still on hers, holding it immobile, and she could feel the sensuous heat from his touch all the way down to her toes. She pressed her lips together to fight back the moan that threatened to escape. How could he overpower her senses in such a way that she couldn't think straight?

Frowning, she blew out an aggravated breath as she pulled her hand from his and resumed what she was doing. "I don't consider it as cleaning up after you, Storm. It's an old habit. Whenever Dad and I ate together, I always cleared the table afterward. We had a deal. He cooked and I cleaned."

"Really?" he asked, studying her intently as his lips quirked into a smile. "And why was that? Can't you cook?"

She glanced up at him and the deep dimples in his cheeks did things to her insides that were totally beyond her comprehension. She figured it would have been a lot easier for her to understand if she wasn't a twenty-six year old virgin. While in college she'd *almost* gone all the way with a senior guy by the name of Tyrone Pembrooke. But his roommate had returned unexpectedly, interrupting things. For her, it had been fortunate since she'd later discovered he had made a bet with his fraternity brothers that he would get into her panties in a week's time. She had almost learned too late that the name the senior guys had given the freshman girls was *fresh meat*.

"Yes, I can cook," she finally answered Storm. "Dad loved home cooking. He thought food wasn't worth eating if it wasn't made from scratch. He just couldn't get into those little microwave dinners that I was an expert at preparing."

Storm chuckled as he helped her gather up the remaining items off the table. "Hey, I can understand your father's pain since I like home-cooked food, too."

They walked over to the garbage container and tossed in their trash. "You cook for yourself every day?" Jayla asked as they headed toward the lower deck to depart.

"No. Since my shifts run twenty-four on and forty-eight off, I eat at the station when I'm working and the days I'm off I eat at Chase's Place, my brother's restaurant."

She nodded, remembering that his twin brother, Chase Westmoreland, owned a restaurant in downtown Atlanta. It was a really popular place; she had been to it several times and always found the food delicious. She glanced down at her watch. "When we get back to the hotel, it will be nap time for me."

"Umm, not for me. There's still more for me to see. I think I'll go check out that club on Bourbon Street that's located right next to the drugstore. I hear they have good entertainment."

Jayla lifted a brow. She knew exactly what club he was referring to, since a group of the guys who'd also attended the convention had visited there. And if what she'd heard about it was true, its only entertainment was of the strip-tease kind. She frowned wondering why the thought of Storm watching women bare all bothered her. Why did men fail to realize that there was more to a woman than what was underneath her clothes?

"Well, I hope you enjoy yourself," she said. Her tone had been more curt than she had intended.

"Oh, trust me, I will."

And she knew, just as clearly as he'd said it, that he would.

Three

Storm was having a lousy time, but when he glanced over at his cousin Ian, it was evident that he was enjoying himself. Ian had contacted him last night and told him that *The Delta Princess* would be making a stop in New Orleans and suggested they meet for drinks at this club.

A few seconds later, Ian must have felt him staring and looked over at him. "What's the matter with you, Storm?"

Storm decided to be honest. "I'm bored."

Ian lifted a brow. "How can you be bored looking at women take off their clothes?"

He shrugged. "It all looks basically the same."

A smile curved the corners of Ian's lips. "Well, yeah, I would hope so."

Storm couldn't help but return the smile. He and Ian were first cousins—their fathers were brothers. While growing up, they had always been close. They were the same age and one thing they'd always had in common was their appreciation of the opposite sex. Storm wasn't surprised that his cousin thought the fact that his lack of interest in women stripping naked was strange.

"Okay, who is she?"

Storm looked confused. "Who's who?"

"The woman who's ruined your interest in other women."

Storm frowned. He glared at Ian. "Where on earth did you get a crazy idea like that from? No one has ruined my interest in other women."

Ian met his glare. "And I say you're lying."

Storm released a frustrated sigh. Ian was damn lucky he hadn't hauled off and hit him. But that was his brother Thorn's style. Thorn was known for his moody, ready-to-knock-the-hell-out-of-you temperament. At least, that had been his attitude until he'd gotten married. Now Tara had unruffled Thorn's feathers and the last few times he'd seen him, Thorn had actually been easygoing. Marriage had certainly made a happy man out of Thorn, as well as his brothers Dare and Stone. Storm found it downright sickening. He'd also been curious as to why his brothers were smiling all the time. As far as he was concerned, they weren't getting anything at home that he wasn't getting out there in the streets.

Or were they?

"I can't believe you just sat there calmly after I called you a liar, so it must be true," Ian said, taking another sip of his beer.

Storm rolled his eyes. "I just don't feel like knocking the hell out of you right now Ian, so back off." What he preferred not to let his cousin know was that he had pretty much hit on the truth. For the time being, Jayla *had* ruined him for other women and he couldn't understand why. He certainly hadn't ever been intimate with her and he never ever intended to be. And yet, here he was bored to death at the sight of these half-clad dancers, while the thought of Jayla taking off her clothes made him break into a sweat.

"Want another drink, cuz?"

He glanced over at Ian. What he wanted was to go back to the hotel and call Jayla to see what she was doing. "No, I'll pass. When will you be back in Atlanta?"

Ian leaned back in his chair and smiled. "In a few weeks. I promised Tara I'd be in town for that charity ball she's working on. Why?"

"I'll check you out then." Storm stood and tossed a couple of bills on the table. "I'll let Uncle James and Aunt Sarah know you're doing okay."

Ian nodded. "And for heaven's sake if Mom asks if I was with a woman when you saw me, please say yes. With your brothers getting married, she's starting to look at us kind of funny."

Storm grinned. His mother was beginning to look at him and Chase kind of funny, too. He glanced around the room before turning his attention back to Ian. "I guess I can tell her that and not feel guilty about lying, since this place is full of women. I'll just leave out the part that the woman you were seeing was naked."

Ian chuckled. "Thanks, I'd appreciate that."

Storm turned to leave.

"Hey, Storm?"

Storm turned back around. "Yeah?"

Ian met his gaze directly. "I know it's just a temporary thing, man, but whomever she is I hope she's worth all the hell you're going through."

Storm frowned, opened his mouth to give his cousin a blazing retort that no woman was putting him through hell, changed his mind and turned and walked out of the club.

Jayla heard the phone ring when she had finished toweling herself off and slipped into the plush hotel bathrobe. She quickly left the bathroom and picked up the phone on the fourth ring. "Hello?"

"How was your nap?"

Jayla frowned. The last thing Storm needed to know was that she hadn't been able to sleep, thanks to thoughts of him being surrounded by naked women. Each time she'd tried closing her eyes, she saw women, taking off their clothes, heaving their breasts in his face, skimming panties down their legs and giving him an eyeful of all their treasures. She'd even heard there were some women who were bold enough to sit naked in a man's lap if he tipped her well enough.

"My nap was fantastic," she lied. "How was the entertainment at the club?" she asked then wished that she hadn't.

"It was definitely interesting."

Jayla's frown deepened. A part of her wanted to slam the phone down, but she had too much pride to do so. Besides, she took great care of herself and thought she looked rather decent, in or out of her clothes. As far as she was concerned, there was nothing those women who'd stripped off their clothes had on her other than that none of them was Adam Cole's daughter.

"I called to see if you're free later."

She rolled her eyes upward. So they were back to that again. "Dinner, you mean?"

"Yes."

In her present frame of mind, he was the last person she wanted to see. It was on the tip of her tongue to suggest he invite one of the "ladies" from the club to dine with him. But she thought better of making the suggestion, since he might very well do it. "I think I'll pass on dinner. I'm not hungry."

"Well, I am, so how about keeping me company?"

She lifted a brow. "Keep you company?"

"Yeah, I enjoy being with you."

Jayla dropped down on the bed, feeling ridiculously pleased by his admission. Although she knew that she shouldn't read too much into his words, she suddenly felt confident, cocky and in control. "Well, I hope you know that my company is going to cost you," she said, breaking the silence between them.

"In what way?"

She rubbed her fingers over the smooth wood-grain texture of the nightstand next to the bed. "I'm not hungry for anything heavy, but I'd love to have a slice of K-Paul's mouthwatering strawberry cheesecake."

She could hear him chuckle on the other end. "K-Paul's Louisiana Kitchen? I've heard of the place, but have never eaten there. I'm going to take your word that I won't be disappointed," he said.

She grinned. "Trust me, you won't be."

"How long will it take for you to get ready?"

"I just got out of the shower so it won't take me long to slip into something."

It was close to forty-five minutes before Jayla appeared in the lobby.

But the moment she walked off the elevator, Storm

knew she had been well worth the wait. His chest grew tight as he watched her walk toward him, thinking she looked absolutely incredible.

He'd known he was in trouble when she had mentioned on the phone that she had just gotten out of the shower. Immediately, visions of her naked had swam his mind, which was a lot better than any live scene he had witnessed at that club earlier.

Common sense told him to pull himself together and remember who she was. But at the moment, all his senses, common or otherwise, were being shot to hell with every step she took toward him. He stood practically unmoving as he watched her, enraptured, while hot desire surged through his bloodstream.

She was dressed in a short dress that totally flowed over her figure, emphasizing the gorgeous shape of her body as well as her long beautiful legs. His gaze lowered slightly to those legs. It had been hard to keep his eyes off them this morning, and it seemed this evening wouldn't be any different. She had the kind of legs any man would just love to caress and have wrapped around him.

He drew in a deep breath, not wanting to think such thoughts but discovering he was hard-pressed to stop them from coming. Whether he liked it or not, he was undeniably attracted to Jayla Cole.

"Sorry I kept you waiting," Jayla said when she came to a stop in front of Storm.

"You were worth the wait. Ready to go?"

"Yes."

They took a cab over to the restaurant and Storm was glad he'd gotten the hotel to make reservations for him. The place was packed. "Something smells delicious," he whispered to Jayla as a waiter showed them to their table.

"Everything in here is delicious," she said smiling.

Including you, Storm was tempted to say. He wondered how he could assume that when he'd never tasted her, but he just knew that she would taste delicious.

The waiter presented them with menus. "Just coffee for me now and I'll wait for later to order dessert," she said handing the menu back to their waiter.

Storm glanced over at her. "Since you're familiar with this place, what do you suggest?"

Jayla caressed her upper lip with the tip of her tongue as if in deep thought. "Umm, I'll have to recommend Chef Paul's Duck & Shrimp Dulac. I had it the last time I was here and it was totally magnificent."

Storm nodded and returned the menu to the waiter. "Then that's what I'll have and I'd like a bottle of sparkling mineral water."

"Great choice, sir," the waiter said before walking off.

Storm leaned back in his chair. "So, do you return to work on Monday?"

Jayla shook her head. "No, I won't officially return to work until a week from Monday. Then on Tuesday of that same week, I have a meeting with a Dr. Tara Westmoreland. Is she a family member of yours?"

Storm smiled. "Yes, Tara is my sister-in-law. She and my brother Thorn tied the knot a few months back. Why would you need to meet with Tara? She's a pediatrician and you don't have a child."

Not yet, Jayla thought to herself. "The reason I'm meeting with Dr. Westmoreland is for business reasons—in fact, we're doing lunch. The company I work for, Sala

Industries, is picking up the tab for the caterers the night that the Kids' World calendar is unveiled at a charity ball, and Dr. Westmoreland is on the committee. It will be a huge event, and we expect well over a thousand people to attend."

"I understand the ball will be next month," he said, after the waiter had returned with their drinks.

"Yes, the second weekend in October, in fact. And I understand your brother Thorn is Mr. July."

"Yes, he is." Storm couldn't forget how Tara had been given the unlucky task of persuading Thorn to pose as Mr. July. Doing so hadn't been easy, but things had worked out in the end, including Thorn's realizing that he loved Tara and the two of them getting married. Kids' World was a foundation that gave terminally ill children the chance to make their ultimate dream—a visit to any place in the world—come true. All proceeds for the foundation came from money raised through numerous charity events.

"I understand the calendar turned out wonderfully and the sale of them will be a huge success," Jayla said smiling, interrupting his thoughts. She gazed across the table at him for a second, then said. "Tell me about your family."

Storm raised a brow after taking a sip of his water. "Why?"

She smiled. "Because I was an only child and whenever you mention your siblings or your cousins I can tell you all share a special closeness. It was lonely growing up without sisters or brothers and I've already made up my mind to have a large family."

Storm chuckled. "How large?"

"At least two, possibly three, maybe even four."

Storm nodded. He wanted a large family as well. "The

Westmoreland family is a big one and we're all very close. It started out with my grandparents who had three sons, one of which was my father. My parents had six kids, all boys until Delaney came along. Dare is the oldest, then Thorn, Stone, Chase and me. As you know, Chase is my twin brother. My father's twin brother's name is James and he and his wife Sarah also had six kids, but all of them were boys—Jared, Spencer, Durango, Ian, Quade and Reggie. My father's youngest brother, Uncle Corey, never married, so it was assumed he'd never fathered any kids, but we discovered differently a few months ago."

Jayla placed her coffee cup down, curious. "Really?"

"His sons, who never knew he was their father, just like he never knew he had sons, had an investigator track him down. Uncle Corey is a retired park ranger in Montana and that's where they found him."

Jayla was fascinated with the story Storm was sharing with her. "But how did he not know that he was a father?"

"It seems a former girlfriend found out she was pregnant after they'd broken up and never bothered telling him. Unknown to Uncle Corey, the woman gave birth to triplets."

"Triplets?"

"Yes, triplets. Multiple births are common in our family. Like me and Chase, Ian and Quade, and my father and Uncle James are fraternal twins."

Jayla inhaled, trying to absorb all this. "And your uncle's former girlfriend had triplets?"

"Yes, the first in the Westmoreland family. It seems that she told them their father had died when they were born and only revealed the truth on her deathbed. Although

Uncle Corey never married the woman, she had moved out west to Texas and had taken his last name, so fortunately, her kids were born as Westmorelands."

"So your Uncle Corey has three sons he didn't know a thing about?"

"No, two sons and one daughter." He shook his head, chuckling. "And all this time we all thought Delaney was the only girl in the Westmoreland family in two generations. Last month Uncle Corey suprised us and got married!"

They suspended conversation when the waiter brought out Storm's food. Storm surprised Jayla when he handed her a fork. "There's too much here for one person. Share it with me."

She glanced at his plate. He did have a lot and it looked delicious. "Umm, maybe, I'll just take a few bites," she said taking the fork from him.

"Help yourself."

And she did. The picture of them sharing a meal played out a rather cozy and intimate scene in her mind, one she tried to ignore. She licked her lips after they had finished. The food had tasted great. "Now you're going to have to help me eat that cheesecake."

"Hey, I can handle it."

His words triggered a flutter in the pit of her stomach. There was no doubt in her mind that Storm Westmoreland could handle anything. And he did. They finished off the strawberry cheesecake in no time.

Storm checked his watch after he signed the check for their bill. "It's still early. How would you like to go dancing?"

His words echoed through Jayla's mind. She knew the smart thing to do would be to tell him, no, but for some reason, she didn't want to think smart. She didn't want to think at all. She was in the company of a very handsome man and she was in no hurry for them to part ways.

She met his gaze. "I'd love going dancing with you, Storm."

The club that had come highly recommend from one of the waiters at K-Paul's was dark, rather small, and crowded. Storm and Jayla were lucky to find an empty table inside Café Basil, which had a reputation of being the undisputed king of nightlife in the French Quarter.

Storm doubted that another couple could fit on the dance floor. Already, the place was jam-packed, but he was determined that they would squeeze in somehow. There was no way he would leave this place tonight without molding Jayla's body to his and holding her in his arms.

He glanced across the table at her, barely able to make out her features in the dimly lit room. Her body was swaying to the sound of the jazz band that was playing and as he watched her, he had to restrain the emotions that were pulsing inside of him.

He had been with numerous women before and each one had met his specific qualifications—whatever they'd been at the time. And every single one of them had known the score. He promised nothing other than a good time in bed. He wasn't interested in satisfying emotional needs, just physical ones. But there was something about Jayla that was pulling at him. The pull was definitely sexual, but there was something about it that was emotional, too.

And Storm Westmoreland didn't do anything with women that hinted of the emotional so why was he here, bursting at the seams to take Jayla into his arms on that dance floor?

Before he could ponder that question, the tune that was playing stopped and another started. Some of the dancers went back to their seats, clearing the way for others to take their turn. "This is our number," he said to Jayla, standing and reaching out for her hand.

She smiled and placed her hand in his. Immediately, he felt a tug in his gut that he tried ignoring as he led her onto the dance floor. He took a deep breath, then exhaled slowly the moment she came into his arms and molded her body to his.

"I like holding you," he said truthfully into her ear moments later, wanting her to hear his words over the sound of the band.

She leaned back and searched his face a moment before asking, "Do you?"

"Hmm…"

She smiled and he thought it was the most beautiful smile he'd ever seen on a woman and felt good that his words had brought a smile to her lips. Speaking of lips…

His gaze shifted to her mouth and he couldn't help but take in their proximity to his. All he had to do was inch a little closer and—

"You smell good, Storm."

He inhaled deeply and slowly shook his head. She could say the damnedest things at times. They should be concentrating on small talk that was socially acceptable for platonic friends and not the sultry murmurings of lovers. "Thanks, but you shouldn't say that to me."

"Why not? If you can tell me that you like holding me, then I should be able to tell you that I think you smell good."

His hands were around her waist, holding her tight, and her arms were draped about his neck. The music playing was slow and their bodies were barely moving. He knew it and she knew it, as well. He was also certain that she was aware that he was aroused. With her body so close to his, there was no way that she didn't know it.

He wanted her to feel all of him and pulled her closer into his arms. Automatically, she placed her head against his chest and he closed his eyes as they swayed to the sound of the music. If she thought he smelled good, then he thought likewise about her. The scent of her perfume was intoxicating, seductive and a total turn-on. Moments later, the music faded and they stopped dancing, but he refused to release her. He needed to continue to hold her in his arms.

Jayla lifted her face and met Storm's gaze. The look in his eyes was intense and purely sexual. "I should try and continue to fight this," he said as if the words were being forced from him. She could clearly understand what he meant.

She did. "Don't fight it," she said softly.

He narrowed his eyes at her. "You're not helping matters, Jayla." His words were a low growl in her ear.

She narrowed her eyes right back at him. "Why should I?"

He stared at her for a long time. Then he glanced around. It seemed they were the center of attention. He looked back at her. "But you deserve more than just—"

"A one-night stand? Shouldn't I be the one to make that decision, Storm? I'm twenty-six-years old. I work and pay my own bills. I'm a woman, not a child, and it's time you realized that."

He stared at her for a long moment, then said, "I just did." He tightened his hand on hers and tugged her along with him out of the club.

* * *

"Where are we going?" Jayla asked, almost out of breath as she tried keeping up with Storm's long strides as he tried hailing a cab.

"Back to the hotel."

A few moments later, Storm cursed. There were few cabs around and the ones he saw were already occupied. He glanced across the street and saw a parked horse-drawn coach. Evidently, someone had used it for a wedding and it reminded him of the coach that might be used as a prop in *Cinderella*. "Come on," he said, keeping a firm hold on Jayla's hand.

They quickly crossed the street and approached the driver, who was holding the reins to keep the horses from prancing. "We need a ride back to the Sheraton Hotel on Canal," Storm said, nearly out of breath.

The old man raised a bushy brow. "My rates are by the hour."

"Fine, just get us there quick and in one piece."

The driver nodded his head, indicating that he understood. Storm then turned and opened the carriage door. When Jayla lifted her leg to climb inside, Storm swept her into his arms and placed her inside on the seat. He then climbed in and shut the door.

As the coach lurched forward, anticipation and sexual desire the likes he had never known before gripped him and he could think of only one thing that could relax him.

He paused, wondering if he had lost his mind and then quickly decided that he had. There wasn't a damn thing he could do about it. He would worry about the consequences of his actions tomorrow. He was too far gone tonight.

He glanced over at Jayla where she sat on the other side of the seat. The interior lighting provided him with barely enough illumination to see her features, but he heard her breathing and it was coming out as erratic as his own.

"Come here, Jayla."

She met his gaze before sliding across the seat to him. He curved his hand about her neck and drew her to him. Leaning forward, he captured the lips he had been dying to taste for over ten years. He took possession and staked his claim. He couldn't help himself.

He felt the shiver that flowed from her body to his when she surrendered her tongue to his. He took his time to savor what she offered, relentlessly mating his mouth with hers as he tried to satisfy what seemed to be an endless hunger. Her taste was like a drug and he felt himself getting addicted to it as his controls were pushed to the limit, wanting more and determined to get it. He lapped up every moan she made while glorying in the feel of her kissing him back.

He deepened the kiss and she proved that she could handle him, tongue for tongue, lick for lick, stroke for stroke. It seemed that he had also tapped a hunger inside of her that she hadn't fed in a while. He intensified the kiss, knowing she wanted him as much as he wanted her.

They felt a jolt when the coach came to a stop and they broke off the kiss, pulling apart. He glanced out the window, then glanced back at her. They were at the hotel. Would she change her mind or would they finish what they'd started?

Knowing the decision was hers, he leaned over and placed a kiss on her lips. "What do you want, Jayla?" he asked, his breath hot and ragged against her ear. He hoped and prayed that she wanted the same thing that he did.

He watched as a smile touched her lips. She then reached out to run her hand down his chest, past his waist to settle firmly on his arousal that was pressing hard through his pants.

He swallowed hard, almost forgetting to breathe. His mind was suddenly filled with scenes of all the things he wanted to do to her.

She met his gaze and in a soft voice whispered, "I want you to make love to me, Storm."

Four

Storm's knuckles gently brushed across Jayla's cheeks just moments before his mouth descended on hers. The words she'd just spoken were what he wanted to hear, and at that moment he needed to taste her again.

He was swamped with conflicting emotions. A part of him wanted to pull back, unable to forget she was Adam's daughter, but then another part of him accepted and acknowledged what she'd said was true. She was old enough to make her own decisions. Even Adam had pretty much conceded that before he'd died.

He slowly, reluctantly, broke off the kiss and took a deep breath. Her eyes glinted with intense desire and he was suddenly filled with a dangerously high degree of anticipation to give her everything she wanted and needed. Without saying a word, he took her hand. Together, they got out of the coach and went into the hotel. The walk across the lobby to the elevator seemed endless, and all Storm could think about was what he would do to her once they were alone. That short dress she was wearing had driven him crazy all night. More than once, his gaze had been drawn to her bare legs, legs he wanted wrapped around him while they made love.

"My room or yours," he asked, moments before the elevator door swooshed open before them.

Their eyes met and held. "Whichever one is closest," she said as desire continued to flicker in her eyes.

"That would be yours."

They stepped into the elevator and after the door closed behind them, he leaned against the wall. They were alone and he tightened his hands by his side. The temptation to pull her into his arms and devour her mouth again was unbearable, and when she swept the tip of her tongue nervously across her top lip, his stomach clenched and he swore beneath his breath.

"I want you so damn much," he had to say. The scent of her perfume was soft and seductive.

"And I want you, too, Storm."

That statement didn't help matters, either. He had wanted to pull her into his arms the moment the elevator came to a stop on her floor, but taking a deep breath, he held the door as she stepped out off the car before him. Holding hands, they walked silently down the corridor to her hotel room. Intense sexual need was closing in on him. He had to admit he'd never wanted a woman this badly.

When they reached her room, he leaned against the wall as Jayla opened her purse, pulled out her key and inserted it into the lock. She opened the door with ease and walked into the room. He didn't waste any time following and closing the door behind them. She flipped a switch that brought a soft glow of light to the room, then turned slowly to him, meeting his gaze.

They didn't say anything for a brief moment; then he reached out and pulled her into his arms. His mind told him to take things slowly but the moment he touched her and desire swept through his body, he threw the thought of taking things slowly out the window. The only thing he could think of was lifting her short dress and becoming enfolded in her feminine heat.

He tightened his arms around her as his mouth greedily devoured hers and his chest expanded with the solid feel of her breasts pressing against it. His tongue again made a claim on her mouth while his hands skimmed across her backside, making him intensely aware of just how shapely she was. He deepened the kiss and a hoarse sound of pleasure erupted from his throat. Moments later, he broke off the kiss and pulled back. He wanted her with an intensity that bordered on desperation.

"You sure?" he asked, wanting to make certain she knew exactly what she was getting into.

"I'm positive," she said, drawing up close to him.

"Hell, I hope so." He pulled her back to him and his mouth came down on hers with a ferociousness that he didn't know he possessed. Fed by the raging storm that had erupted within him, his mouth plundered hers, sweeping her breath away and tasting the sweet, deep and delicious taste that was distinctively hers. He felt the tremor that passed through her and it increased his need to make love to her to the point where his veins throbbed.

Storm lifted his head just long enough to reach out and whip the short dress over Jayla's head, leaving her standing before him clad in a silky black camisole. He suddenly became dizzy with the sight of her standing before him, lush and sexy. Her scent was seductive and the pale lighting in the room traced a faint glow across her dark skin. His temperature went up another notch and he knew at that moment what he was about to share with Jayla went way beyond his regular routine of "wham-bam, thank you, ma'am." And for a mere second, that thought bothered him. But like everything else that was out of the norm for him tonight, he placed it on the back burner. He'd deal with his confusing thoughts tomorrow.

He reached out and pulled her back to him, capturing her mouth at the same time he picked her up in his arms and walked toward the bed. He placed her in the center of it and tumbled down beside her, his hands immediately going to her camisole to remove it from her body.

He sucked in air through clenched teeth when he pulled back and looked down at her, completely naked. At that moment he felt an unbearable desire to feel his mouth on her skin. Leaning toward her, his tongue traced a path down her neck to her breasts, where it stopped and drew a hard, budding nipple into his mouth and feasted, licking, sucking.

He felt her tremble again and heard the purring sound that came from deep within her throat. She wanted more and was letting him know it. He took his hand and ran it across the flat of her stomach, moving lower until he found the moist heat of her. He touched her there, glorying in her dampness. Deftly, expertly, his fingers went to work.

Jayla felt her breath rushing in and out of her lungs. Although there was light in the room and her eyes were open, she felt her world was on the edge of blackness. She felt light-headed, dizzy, dazed, and she was feeling things that she'd never felt before. Storm's fingers were driving her out of her mind, and what his mouth was doing to her breasts was pure torture. Her body felt hot, on fire, in need of something it had never had before, but something it desperately needed.

She groaned deep in her throat. It was either that or scream out loud. So she clamped her mouth shut, but couldn't stop from releasing a sound that was alien to her ears. At the moment, nothing mattered but the feel of Storm's mouth and hands on her.

"I can't wait any longer," she heard him say, as he eased away from her. She watched as he stood next to the bed and quickly removed his shirt, almost tearing off the buttons in the process. Then he wasted no time in removing his pants and briefs. She continued to watch him when, with the expertise of a man who had done it many times before, he ripped the condom from the packet he had taken from his pant pockets and slid it over his erection.

She blinked at the size of him and before she could form the words to let him know of her virginal state, he had returned to the bed, pulled her into his arms and captured her mouth with his, once again giving in to the thirst of her desire; a desire that only he could quench. Want and need spiraled through her, making blood pump fast and furious through her veins. It seemed his mouth and hands were everywhere. Her insides were churning, her stomach was spinning and her brain had turn to mush. She didn't know what was driving him, but whatever the source, it was driving her, too. She felt the tip of his erection pressing against the entrance to her feminine mound in such a way that beckoned her to part her legs for him.

Then he kissed her again, long, hard, as his tongue plowed hers in breath-stealing strokes. She savored all the things he was doing to her, all the ways he was making her feel and wondered if the feelings would ever end, hoping and praying that they wouldn't, yet at the same thing knowing there was something else she needed, something she had to have.

She felt him place his body over hers, felt the strength of his thighs entwining with hers and relished the strong beat of his heart against her breasts. He lifted her hips into his hands.

He broke off their kiss and met her gaze, looked down at her the moment he pushed himself inside of her, with one deep, hard thrust. Her body stiffened and she gasped as a surge of pain ripped through her.

He immediately went still as total disbelief lined his features. "Jayla?"

Her name was a low rumble from deep within his throat. She saw the shock that flared in his eyes and felt the tension coiling within him. A spurt of panic swept through her at the thought that he wouldn't finish what he'd started, so she decided to take action.

"Don't ask," she said, then leaned upward and recaptured his mouth with hers. Her hands clutched at his shoulders and her legs wrapped solidly around him, locking him in place. She felt his resistance and began kissing him in all the ways he had kissed her that night, letting her tongue tangle relentlessly with his. He slowly began moving, easing in and out her, claiming her, taking her, making love to her in a way she always dreamed that lovemaking was supposed to be. The only thought on her mind was the strength of him driving back and forth, rocking her world and send-

ing her over the edge. She knew she would remember every
moment of this night for as long as she lived.

A groan eased from Storm's lips as Jayla's body met his,
stroke for stroke. His hand reached down and lifted her hips
to him for a closer fit, as if they weren't already close
enough. She was tight, sensuously so, and his body surged
in and out of hers, back and forth, massaging her insides
the same way and with the same rhythm that her breasts
were massaging his chest.

He had recovered from shock at discovering she'd been
a virgin and decided since he was the one initiating her into
lovemaking, that he would do it right. And the little whim-
pering sounds coming from her lips told him that he was
definitely making an impact.

"Storm…"

He felt her body jerk at the same time she pressed her
head into his shoulder to stifle a scream. The intensity of
her climax jolted him, nearly stealing his breath before he
followed her in his own release, yanked into the strongest
and most mindless orgasm he had ever experienced in his
entire life. And it was destined to be the longest…or perhaps he was having multiples, back to back. There was no
way to tell since the earth-shattering sensations were hitting him all at once in every form and from every possible
angle. The feeling was unique, incredible, out of this world
and once in a lifetime. He hadn't expected this and was
caught off guard by the magnitude of what was happening
to him. He was being hurled into something he had never
before experienced.

"Jayla!"

Her name was torn from his lips and he threw his head
back as he continued to pump rapidly into her when he felt

another climax claim him—his third, possibly a fourth. With a growl that came low from deep within his throat, he leaned down and pressed a kiss to her mouth as his body continued to tumble into oblivion, and he knew what they had shared was nothing short of heaven.

"I did as you requested and didn't ask then, but I'm asking now, Jayla."

Storm's words gave her pause. She let out a deep breath and wondered why he couldn't be one of those men who just accepted things as they were?

She looked up at him and saw the intensity in the depth of his dark eyes. She also saw the impressive shape of his lips and his well-toned, broad chest that was sprinkled with dark curly hair. And it wasn't helping matters that they were both naked in bed, with him leaning on his elbow and looming over her. She closed her eyes and shook her head. The man was too handsome for his own good…or for hers.

"Tell me," he whispered, then leaned down and placed a soft kiss on her bare shoulder. "Tell me why, in this day and age, a twenty-six year old woman would still be a virgin."

She met his gaze. "Because women in this day and age have choices," she said slowly, then asked. "Have you ever taken a love compatibility quiz?"

Storm arched his brow. "A what?"

She smiled at the confused look on his face. "A love compatibility quiz. There's a site on the Internet where you can go and take this quiz if you're looking for Mr. or Miss Right. Well, after a few dates with losers—men who lacked confidence but had plenty of arrogance and who also acted as if it was a foregone conclusion that our date would end in my bed—I decided to take the quiz and my results indicated that my Mr. Right didn't exist."

Storm frowned down at her. Would he ever understand women? "You've been avoiding a serious relationship because of some quiz?"

"Pretty much…yes. I discovered like oil and water, me and relationships don't mix because I have a low tolerance when it comes to men who expect too much too soon."

It took Storm a minute to analyze everything she'd said. "What about those guys you dated off the Internet?"

Jayla released a single, self-deprecating chuckle. "That was my way of trying to prove the quiz wrong. From then on, I never wasted my time going on a guy hunt."

"But…but didn't you date in college?" Storm sputtered. Why hadn't her going off to college assured her returning to town with her hymen no longer intact?

She smiled again, a bit sadly this time. "Yes, but unfortunately, not long after I got there I met a guy name Tyrone Pembroke."

"What happened? He broke your heart?"

She chuckled derisively. "On the contrary. Actually he did me a favor by showing me just what jerks some guys were. He opened my eyes to the games they played, games I wasn't interested in. After Ty, I made it a point not to get serious about any one guy and since I wasn't into casual sex, I never felt pressured into sleeping with anyone."

Storm nodded. "So why now and why with me?

To Jayla's way of thinking, that was an easy question. "Because of timing. I know you and I like you. I also know your position on relationships. I'm not looking for anything beyond what we shared tonight and neither are you, right?"

Storm held her gaze. "Right." The last thing he needed

was a clingy woman who wanted to occupy his time. Still, although he didn't want to feel it, he felt a special connection to Jayla since he had been her first. He couldn't recall ever taking a woman's virginity before.

"Now that I've answered your question, do you think I can get some sleep? I'm exhausted." Jayla asked softly.

Storm glanced down at her. Was she dismissing him? "Do you want me to leave?"

She smiled. "Actually…" she began, as she snuggled closer to him. "I was hoping you'd want to stay all night."

A grin spread across Storm's lips. Hell, yeah, he wanted to stay all night. "I think that can be arranged," he told her as he leaned down and placed a kiss on her lips. "Excuse me for a second while I go into the bathroom to take care of something. I'll be right back."

"All right."

There was just enough light in the darkened room to let Jayla admire Storm's nude form as he crossed the room to the bathroom. She inhaled deeply as heated sensations shot through her. He'd been the perfect lover. He was confident, secure in who he was, but not arrogant. She felt tired and yet exhilarated at the same time. Slightly sore, but still smoldering from his lovemaking. Funny how things worked out. Storm was the man she'd been trying to get to notice her since the time she had started noticing boys. She was beginning to believe the cliché that good things came to those who wait. Now timing had not only finally worked for them, it was working against them as well. At any other time, she would have loved to take what she'd shared with Storm tonight to a whole other level, but not now. What she had needed was him out of her system so she could focus on the baby.

Her baby.

"I'm back."

Her nipples peaked in instant response to his words. She watched as he made a casual stroll over to the bed, totally at ease with his naked state. Seeing him that way stirred up desires within her again and she no longer felt as tired as she had earlier.

"Do you want me to prepare you some bath water to soak in for a while before you go off to sleep?" he asked coming to sit on the side of the bed next to where she lay. "If you don't, you might wake up feeling a lot sorer than you probably do now."

Jayla leaned back against her pillow, seriously doubting that most men were as considerate as Storm was being. She pressed her lips together, liking his suggestion. "You're right, a soak in the tub sounds wonderful."

He smiled as he stood up. "I'll be back when your bath is ready."

"All right."

Again she watched him cross the room, finding it hard to tear her gaze from the sight of him, especially his tight behind. She smiled, feeling downright giddy at the thought that he'd agreed to spend the night with her. She might as well stretch this out for as far as she could because when they returned to Atlanta, things would be different. She would go her way and he would go his. They would both resume a life that had nothing to do with each other. He would go back to being a hero by fighting his fires and saving lives and she would eagerly prepare for the most life-altering experience she'd ever encountered—pregnancy.

"Ready?"

Hearing the sound of his voice, she glanced across the

room. A thick surge of desire shot through her veins at the sight of him leaning in the doorway, naked and aroused. If she wasn't ready, he certainly was.

"Yes, I'm ready," she said, barely able to voice the words. She moved to get out of bed and then he was there, sweeping her up into his arms. The heat of his skin seeped through the heat of hers and the feeling was electrifying. She immediately knew the meaning of the words *raging hormones*. Hers were totally out of control. She quickly decided that she needed to get back in control of things.

"I can walk, Storm."

"Yes, but I want to carry you. That's the least I can do."

She clamped her lips tight, deciding not to tell him that he had done quite a lot. He had turned their night into more than a one-night stand. It had become a romantic interlude, one she would remember for the rest of her life.

As he carried her into the bathroom, her breasts tingled from the contact with his skin. And when he leaned down, shifting her in his arms to place her into the bubbly water, sliding her body down his, the sensations that rocketed through her almost took her breath away.

"The water might be a little warmer than what you're used to, but it will be good for your muscles," he said, in a voice that let her know he, too, had been affected by the contact of their bare skin touching.

She nodded as he placed her in the water. He was right. The water was warm, but it immediately felt good to her body. She glanced up at him as he stood beside the tub looking down at her. She tried to keep her attention on the top part of his body and not the lower part. "You seem to be good at this, Westmoreland. Is this how you treat all your virgins?"

He chuckled and his gaze captured hers. "Believe it or not, I've never done a virgin before."

She lifted a brow. "Never?"

His smile widened. "No. never. You're my first, just like I was your first."

Jayla watched as his features shifted into a serious expression as if he had to really think about what he'd just said for a moment. "Do you need my help?" he asked her.

She shook her head. "No, I can manage. Thanks."

He nodded. "Call me when you're ready to get out."

She smiled. "Storm, really, I can manage things."

"Yeah, I know you can but I want you to call me anyway." Then he left, closing the door behind him.

Storm poured himself a glass of ice water and tipped it to his mouth, wishing it was something stronger but appreciating the cool liquid as it soothed his dry throat.

He had sworn off having anything to do with Jayla years ago; yet now, after finally making love to her, he was aching so badly for her again that it actually hurt. To make matters worse, the taste of her was still strong on his tongue and, before he could contain himself, he groaned, which was followed by a growl that erupted from deep within his throat. Jayla Cole had no idea just what a desirable and sexy woman she was. Even being a novice at making love, she was every man's fantasy. He could see her attracting the wrong kind of men and felt a heartfelt sense of pride, as well as relief, that she had kept her head on straight and had not been taken in by any of them.

But was he any better? His no-commitment, hands-on-but-hearts-off, no-strings-attached policy left a lot to be desired, but he and Jayla had been struck by that unique kind of passion that had sent her straight into his arms and had propelled him unerringly into her bed.

And he had no regrets.

Frowning, Storm took another huge swallow of water. No woman had ever gotten to him like this. It was time for him to start building a defense to the passion she aroused in him. He pulled on his pants and did his best to reorder his chaotic thoughts and unruly emotions.

He heard a sound and turned around. Jayla was standing in the doorway wearing one of the hotel's complimentary bathrobes. His heart fluttered as he assessed her from head to toe. She looked refreshed. She looked incredible, blatantly sexy. With a steadying breath, he asked, "Why didn't you call me when you were ready to get out of the tub?"

She smiled and his pulse kicked up a notch. "Because although I was tempted, it wouldn't be a good idea to start becoming dependent on you."

For him, it wasn't an issue of dependency. He'd known she could manage on her own but he had wanted to be there to help her anyway. There was something about her that pulled at his protective instincts…among other things. "Do you feel better?"

"Yes," Jayla said, blowing out a ragged breath as her gaze roamed over him, noticing that he had put his pants back on. What a shame. She was beginning to get used to seeing him naked.

She met his gaze again and couldn't help but notice that his eyes were dark, very dark, and her body's reaction to it was spontaneous. "I, ah, need to get a nightgown out the drawer," she said in a voice that sounded soft and husky even to her ears. She swallowed deeply when he slowly crossed the room to her.

"Have you ever slept in the nude?" he said, reaching out, opening her robe and sliding his hands over her bare skin, beginning with her waist, moving to her hips and then reaching around to cup her bottom.

"Ah, no," she said, barely getting the words out.

He gave her that killer smile. "Would you like to try it? I can't think of anything I'd like better than to have your naked body next to mine all night."

A small purring sound left Jayla's throat when he leaned forward and his tongue licked the area underneath her right ear, then the left. A sensuous shudder ran all through her, and she thought that a woman could definitely become dependent on his kind of treatment. And then she ceased to think at all when he stopped messing around with her ears and shifted his focus, opening his mouth hotly over hers.

Images of how intimate they'd been less than an hour ago flooded her mind. They had been together in bed with him on top of her, their legs entwined, their bodies connected while making love the same way they had done numerous times in her dreams. But this was no dream; it was reality. And the scent of his body heat and the sound of his breathing while he was kissing her did more than stir up her desire; it was stroking her with an intensity that shook her to the core, forging past those emotions she kept tightly guarded.

The thought that Storm was seeping through the barriers she'd set around her emotions disturbed Jayla, but she was too absorbed in the way his tongue was stroking the insides of her mouth to worry about it. This kiss was so full of greed and sensuality that she could feel the air crackling around them, and she was returning with equal vigor everything he was putting into their kiss.

And then slowly, reluctantly, he pulled back and his gaze locked to hers. "So, do we get naked?"

She swallowed. The huskiness in his voice made her want to do a lot more than get naked. "Yes," she managed to get out in a shaky breath.

"Good," he murmured, then reached up and pushed the robe off her shoulders, letting it fall in a heap at her feet. "Let's go back to bed."

Taking her hand into his, he lifted it to his lips and placed a warm kiss against the center of her palm. And then he picked her up in his arms and carried her to the bed. He placed her in the middle and then stood back to remove his pants.

Jayla watched him while thinking that nothing, other than a fire alarm going off, could distract her at that moment. She wanted to see every inch of him again, especially that part that had given her so much pleasure. He kept his gaze on her as he slowly eased down his pants. Then she watched as he pulled a condom packet out of his pants and went through the process of sheathing himself.

When he had finished, he glanced over at her and smiled. "Although I don't plan for us to do anything but sleep, there's nothing wrong with playing it safe."

She sighed and it took a lot of effort to concentrate on his words and not on him. "Umm, yes, that's smart thinking."

He quickly got into the bed, pulled her into his arms and felt her shiver. "You're cold?" he asked in a low, husky voice.

She shook her head. "No, quite the contrary. I'm hot."

He smiled. "I know a way to cool you off," he said, shifting his position to reach down between her legs to slide his fingers back and forth through her feminine curls.

She closed her eyes and moaned as he slowly but thoroughly began stroking a fire within her. "I—I don't think that's helping, Storm," she murmured, barely able to get the words out.

"Sure it is," he whispered close to her ear. "Just relax, feel and enjoy."

And she did.

His fingers literally drove her crazy. The sensation of his fingertips as they intimately skimmed her feminine folds at a sensuously maddening and erratic pace had her purring and moaning.

She made the mistake of opening her eyes and meeting his gaze. Something she saw in the depths of his eyes took her breath away. Her senses suddenly became filled with an emotion that caused a tightening in her chest at the same time that her body lost control, exploded. The sensations that shot through her made her cry out, call his name and then he was capturing her mouth with his, kissing her deeply while he continued to skim the tip of his fingers between her legs.

Moments later, she felt her body become weak and she could barely reclaim her breath as he cuddled her limp body next to his, holding her tightly. She knew if she wasn't careful, that she was going to fall—

No! She couldn't go there. She couldn't even think such a thing. The only thing she wanted to focus on was how he was making her feel. She had made plans for her future and Storm Westmoreland wasn't a part of those plans. But here, now, at this very moment, he was part of her present and was giving her undiluted pleasure. She could not refuse what he was offering and when they parted in two days, she would always have these memories.

Five

Storm drew in a long breath as he looked down at the woman asleep in his arms. His chest tightened and he forced back the surge of desire that swept through him. She was an unbelievably beautiful woman.

Bathed in the rays of predawn light that spilled through the hotel's window, Jayla's hair, a glossy medium brown with strands of golden highlight, was spread across the pillow and shone luxuriously against the darkness of her creamy skin.

Sharing a bed with her hadn't been easy. In fact, he doubted that he'd gotten any sleep. While trying to find that perfect sleeping position, she had twisted and turned most of the night. And he had been tormented with each and every move she'd made. At one time, she had lain facing him, with her leg thrown over his, with his arousal pressing against her center.

Then there had been that time when she had shifted around, placing her back to his chest, her sweet delectable backside right smack up against his groin. More than once during the course of the night he had been tempted to just say, "To hell with it," and ease inside of her. His mind had been filled with numerous possibilities. Instead, he had fought the urge and had wrapped his arms around her waist, pulled her close and thought about the time when he *had* been inside of her.

He would never forget how it felt, the moment he'd realized that she was a virgin. At first he'd been shocked, stunned and then panic had set in. But the notion of ending their lovemaking session had fled his mind when she pulled his mouth down to hers and kissed him with a hunger that he had quickly reciprocated.

And now he wanted her again. If truth were told, he hadn't stopped wanting her but had held back to give her body time to adjust to him. Now he was driven with an undeniable need to bury himself deep within her welcoming warmth again. He glanced over at the clock. It was just past six. He wanted to let her sleep but couldn't. He had to have her. Now.

He leaned over, close to her lips. "Jayla?" he whispered. A few moments later, she purred his name and slowly lifted one drowsy eye. Then she opened the other eye and blinked, as if to bring his face into focus.

"Storm," she murmured in a voice that was muffled with sleep, but to his way of thinking sounded sensuous as hell. Little tendrils of hair had drifted onto her face and graced one of her cheeks. He pushed the hair back from her face before sliding that same hand down the length of her body. Shifting slightly, he wanted her to feel his arousal pressing against the curve of her pelvis.

"I want you," he whispered and wondered if she could hear the urgency in his tone. The need. The desperation. She must have because she inched her lips closer to his for him to take control of her mouth, mate with it.

And he did.

His every muscle, his every nerve, felt sensitized as their tongues tangled with a hunger that was driving him crazy. The sweet, honeyed taste of her consumed his mind, sent a flame through his body and made him quickly lose touch with reality.

"Storm," she said softly, breaking off their kiss as her hands reached down, tentatively searching for him. When she captured him in the warmth of her hands, he thought he had died and gone to heaven. "I want this."

He definitely knew what she was asking for and didn't waste any time rolling her beneath him. He reached down and touched her, finding her hot, wet and ready. Lowering his head he needed to taste her breasts and drew one hardened nipple into his mouth, gently pulling it with his tongue, glorying in the shivers he felt going through her.

And then with her hands still holding him, she placed him at her opening and, slanting her hips upward, began easing him inside her. At this stage of the game, his arousal didn't know the meaning of slow and he pushed deep inside, finding her body still tight, but not as tight as it had been the night before. He stopped to give her time to adjust to him, but her soft moans and the rotation of her hips let him know she didn't want him to stop.

He thrust harder, buried himself to the depth they both wanted, and then he kissed her again, needing the contact to her mouth. And then he began to move inside of her as intense, dizzying, mind-boggling desire consumed him, sending him on a voyage that was out of this world. And Jayla was right there, taking the trip with him, as they flew higher and higher to the place where passion was taking them. A place that was a potent blend of exultation and euphoria, a place where he wanted to think that few people went—at least not to this degree and certainly not this level.

"Wow," he whispered huskily, for lack of a better word, and then he increased his pace, established their rhythm and like finely tuned musical instruments they played together in absolute harmony. Each movement added sensation and increased their pleasure. He dragged in a deep breath, feeling as if he were seconds from toppling over the edge, moments from exploding.

He clamped his hands down on her hips while he mated relentlessly with her. Her feminine muscles began gripping, clutching him with every thrust he took. And when he heard the sharp cry that was torn from her lips and felt her body jolt at the same time she arched her back, then shattered in his arms, he let go and began drowning in his own release.

"Jayla!"

He threw his head back, as something, everything, inside him broke free. If he thought he'd experienced pure, unadulterated ecstasy inside her body before, then this was a pleasure so raw and primitive that he doubted he would ever be able to recover from it. It was as if this was where he belonged, where he was supposed to be.

He quickly banished those thoughts from his mind as they continued to move together. He felt as if every cell within him was electrified, energized as they were propelled even deeper into the sensuous clutches that held them.

And then, before they could recover, it happened again,

just as fast and just as potent. They were hurled into another orgasm so powerful that he actually felt the room spin and wondered if he would ever regain his equilibrium. A cry tore from his throat, only to be drowned out by the sound of hers as once again they were plunged into the throes of pure ecstasy.

With a shuddered sigh, he pulled her closer to him, felt himself getting hard all over again and knew this woman was doing more than draining his body. She was draining his very soul and at the moment, he couldn't do a damn thing to stop her.

Jayla couldn't move, so she lay still, feeling sated, exhausted and caught up in the aftereffects of remarkable sex. She stared up at the ceiling as she tried to calm the rhythm of her breathing. She smiled as she forced herself onto her side and faced Storm. He was lying flat on his back with his eyes closed. He, too, took long, deep, steadying breaths. When she saw he was once again aroused, the sight of him sent her senses into a mindless sensuous rush all over again. He was as hard as a rock, seemingly ready for another round. How on earth was that possible?

She sighed deeply. "Everything I've heard about you is true, Storm." She watched as he slowly lifted his eyes, slightly turned his head and looked over at her.

"What have you heard about me?"

Every bone in her body felt as if it had melted, so she chuckled huskily. "That you're perfect in bed. Did you know some women call you, The Perfect Storm?"

Storm frowned. For some reason he didn't want her to think about the other women he'd been with. And he didn't want to think about them, either. The only woman he wanted to think about was her. Instead of answering her question, he leaned over and kissed her deeply, thoroughly, and moments later, when he pulled back, he reached down and touched her intimately. "I didn't mean to be rough."

A huge smile touched the corners of her lips. "You weren't. I got everything I asked for and then some."

"Yeah, but you're new at this."

"And enjoying every minute." She studied him for a moment, then said. "I was curious about you when I was sixteen. You were the first guy I was really interested in."

"Was I?"

"Yes."

Storm held her gaze. He could vividly recall how, whenever he dropped by to visit Adam, her whiskey-colored eyes would seek him out and convey her every youthful emotion. She'd had a crush on him. He had been aware of it and he had a feeling that Adam had been aware of it as well. Storm had known that around her he would have to tread lightly, because she was the boss's daughter who was noticing boys for the first time; but unfortunately, instead of a boy, she had set her sights and budding desires on a man. To make matters worse, she fully intended for him to notice her and he had tried like hell not to.

"Do we stay in bed for the rest of the day or do we get up and do something else?" she asked, interrupting his stroll down memory lane. "Just to let you know, the thought of staying in bed all day doesn't bother me."

Storm couldn't help but laugh. "What have I created here, a monster?"

She lifted a brow. "Like you can talk. I'd say you're up for it," she said, pointing out his aroused state.

"Well, yeah, but some things can't be rushed. Just give me some time, will you."

"Sure, if you think you need it, but from what I understand most men need time to get it up, not down."

One corner of Storm's mouth lifted. He was enjoying this turn in their conversation, but he knew if they didn't get out of bed really soon, their conversation might turn into something else. Forcing himself to move, he slowly sat up. "I guess I need to go back to my room and take a shower." He glanced over at the clock. "Do you want to meet me downstairs for breakfast?"

"Yeah, I'm starving."

He nodded knowingly. "And after breakfast, how about if we do some more sightseeing today?" *Anything to keep them out of their hotel rooms.* "When does your flight leave tomorrow?" he asked. Suddenly, reality of how short their time together would be began to seep in. From the expression on her face he could tell that she felt it, too.

"In the morning, around eight. What about yours?"

"Tomorrow evening, around three."

She nodded. "Too bad we aren't on the same flight," she said quietly.

He'd been thinking the same thing. "Yeah, it's too bad." But then, maybe it was for the best. Too much more of Jayla Cole would go to his head and right to a place he wasn't quite ready for.

He sighed deeply. So much had happened between them in the last forty-eight hours. "Nothing has changed, right Jayla? Neither of us is looking for a serious relationship."

Jayla glanced at him, understanding his need to reestablish ground rules. "Yeah, right, nothing has changed. Trust me, a serious relationship with anyone is the last thing I want or need right now. I'm going to be so busy over the next few months that an involvement of any kind will be the furthest thing from my mind."

He lifted a brow as he slid out of bed. "Oh? What will you be doing?"

Jayla nervously licked her lips. There was no way she could tell him that she would be preparing for motherhood. "There's this project that I'm going to start working on."

"Oh, and what kind of project is it?"

She sighed deeply; he would ask. She decided to brush off his question and forced out a chuckle, saying, "Nothing you'd be interested in, trust me."

He smiled as he studied her for a long moment, then said. "I might surprise you. If you ever need my help, don't hesitate to call."

She smiled. "Thanks for the offer, but I have everything under control."

"All right. I'll be back in a second."

She watched as he walked into the bathroom and closed the door. She rolled over on her stomach and buried her face in his pillow, enjoying his lingering scent. Had she been dreaming or had Storm just offered to help with her project? She felt it was pretty safe to assume that the last thing Storm Westmoreland would want was to be a daddy. Besides, she had no regrets in going solo. A man like him as the father of her child would definitely cramp her style. He'd already stated his belief that a woman couldn't work outside the home *and* raise a family. She didn't envy the woman he would end up marrying, since it was evident that he would be a controlling husband.

She got out of bed, slipped into her robe, walked over to the window and glanced out to watch the impending sunrise. Tomorrow, she and Storm would bring an end to their short affair and she hoped when they returned to Atlanta that they didn't run into each other anytime soon. It would be difficult to see him and not think about the intimacy they had shared here in The Big Easy. There definitely wouldn't be anything easy about that.

Storm slid his hands around Jayla's waist and pulled her snugly against him. "An hour?" he asked with a puzzled lift of his brow. "Are you saying it will take you an entire hour to pick out an outfit for tonight?"

She smiled up at him. "Yes. Already I see a number of things in this dress shop that I want to try on. It has to be just perfect."

"Jayla," he began, but she cut him off.

"Please, Storm. I want a new outfit for tonight."

He studied the excitement in Jayla's face, thinking she was even more beautiful than before, if that were possible. When he had met her for breakfast, he'd told her of the phone call he had received from his cousin Ian. Ian, a good friend of New Orleans's mayor, had been invited to a huge gala being given in the man's honor. Ian had invited Storm as his guest and Storm had gotten the okay to bring Jayla as his date. Instead of going sightseeing as they had originally planned, Jayla had insisted that the first thing she needed to do was go shopping for something to wear that night.

"All right, I guess I can find something to kill time while you shop," he said releasing her. "But I'll be back in a hour, Jayla."

She grinned, nodding. "And I'll have everything I need by then."

A short while later, Storm took his time as he strolled

around Jackson Square. It was a beautiful day and a lot of tourists were out and about. He smiled when he thought of how excited Jayla had been when he'd mentioned tonight's affair. He had enjoyed seeing her happy. He was also enjoying her company…almost a little too much. She was definitely someone he liked being with, both in and out of bed. More than once he had to remind himself not to make more of what they were sharing than there was.

It was no big deal that over the past few days, they'd discovered that they enjoyed many of the same things. She liked jazz, and so did he; she enjoyed watching bone-chilling thriller movies and so did he. She was one of the few people who lived in Atlanta whose favorite football team *wasn't* the Atlanta Falcons. His favorite team was the Dallas Cowboys and she was a fan of the Philadelphia Eagles.

It seemed the only thing they didn't agree on was his belief that a woman's place was at home raising her kids and not in an office all day. Jayla insisted that a man who held such traditional views would be too controlling in a marriage. He didn't see himself as wanting to control, but rather he saw himself as someone who wanted to be the sole provider for his family in the purest sense of the word.

He glanced at his watch. He still had over forty-five minutes to go before he went back to that dress shop for Jayla. Damn, but he missed her already. A warning bell suddenly went off in his head. He'd never admitted to missing a woman before, so why was he doing it now? He sighed deeply, deciding to be honest with himself. The honest truth was he liked having Jayla around and for him that didn't bode well.

He frowned as he continued to walk around Jackson Square, wondering what was there about her that was getting to him and playing games with his mind? They were games he had no desire to play. She knew the score and so did he. Neither of them wanted anything beyond what they were sharing here in New Orleans. Getting together and developing some sort of relationship when they returned to Atlanta was unacceptable, totally out of the question, a definite bad idea.

Then why was he allowing such thoughts to invade his mind?

"You're confused, aren't you?"

Storm turned to the sound of the craggy voice and saw an old woman sitting on the bench less than five feet from where he stood. He lifted a brow. "Excuse me. Did you say something?"

The old woman smiled serenely. "Yes. I said you're confused. Nothing like this has ever happened to you before has it?"

Storm tilted his head to the side as he studied the woman, wondering if she was operating with a full deck. She was talking as if she knew him. "I think you might have me mixed up with someone else."

"No, I don't," she muttered with a shake of her head. "And I'm not crazy," she said, as if reading his mind. "I'd tell you more if you let me look into your future."

Storm nodded as understanding dawned. The old woman was a fortune-teller. New Orleans was full of them. He crossed his arms over his chest amused. "And what do you think you can tell me that I don't already know?"

"Oh, you'd be surprised."

Storm didn't think so but decided to humor the old woman. "Okay, then surprise me. What do you have to work with? Tarot cards or a crystal ball?"

The older woman met his gaze and looked at him with a scrutiny that Storm found unnerving. Finally, she responded. "Neither. I'm a palm reader."

Storm nodded. *That figured.* "Okay, how much to read my palm?"

"Twenty dollars."

He sighed as he reached into his pocket and pulled a twenty-dollar bill while wondering why he was wasting his time. He glanced at his watch. He still had a good thirty minutes left before Jayla was ready and having his palm read was just as good as anything else to pass the time away.

He sat down next to the woman on the bench and stretched out his hand to her. "Okay, what does my palm say?"

He watched as the woman took his hand into her frail one and studied his palm. Moments later, when she lifted her gaze, the intensity in the depth of her dark eyes almost startled him. She smiled sympathetically. "I can see why you're confused."

He frowned. "Meaning what?"

"You are about to make unexpected changes in your life and although you yearn for peace, turbulence is in your future. Keep your sights high, be patient and let destiny take its course."

Storm's frown deepened. He had just gotten a promotion three months ago, so what changes was the woman talking about? He had thought about moving out of his present house and buying a larger one, but what problems could a decision like that bring on? There had to be more.

He lifted his brow. "Is that it?"

She stared at him and sighed deeply. "Trust me, son. That will be enough."

He shook his head, a part of him found the entire thing outright amusing. "Ahh, can you be a little more specific?"

"No, I've told you everything you need to know."

He slowly stood. He couldn't wait until he and his brothers had their next card game so he could tell them about this experience. Knowing them, they would probably find the whole thing hilarious. "Well, it was nice getting my palm read," he said, not knowing what else to say.

She shook her head slowly. "I wish you the best of luck."

Storm looked at the woman. She'd said it like she had truly meant it. "Thanks," he said before walking off, not sure just what he was thanking her for.

"Tell her you like the red one."

He turned back around and lifted a brow. "Excuse me?"

The old woman smiled. "Tell her you like the red one the best."

Storm frowned, not understanding what she meant. He decided it would be best not to ask, so he nodded, turned back around and kept walking. Moments later, when he returned to the dress shop, he saw Jayla standing at the checkout counter waiting for him. His face lit into a smile as he walked over to her. "Did you find anything?"

"Yes," she answered excitedly. "I found two really nice outfits and they're both beautiful. I want you to pick out the one you like the best."

He watched as she turned and grabbed two dresses off the counter, one blue and the other red. Storm blinked twice and his throat suddenly went dry when he remembered what the old woman had said. *Tell her you like the red one.* He stared at the two outfits that Jayla was holding up in front of her.

"Well, which do you like the best, Storm?" she asked, looking from one dress to the other.

"The red one," he replied promptly, feeling somewhat dazed, like he was a participant in *The Twilight Zone*.

Jayla didn't notice his consternation as she handed the red dress to the smiling saleswoman behind the counter. A huge grin touched her lips. "I like the red one best, too."

Later that night, Storm had to admit that he definitely liked the red dress, especially on Jayla. His tongue had nearly fallen out of his mouth the moment she had stepped off the elevator to meet him in the lobby.

Instantaneous. Immediate. A jolt of mind-wrenching desire had shot straight to his groin. There was nothing like an eye-catching, incredulously sexy, tight-fitting dress on a woman who definitely had sleek and delectable curves. Her silver accessories made her look sophisticated, elegant and hot, all at the same time. The dress was short, really short, but then she had legs that transformed the dress from provocative to mind-blowing. Her breasts sat high and looked full, lush and ready to tumble out of the low-cut neckline at any given moment.

"I had a lot of fun tonight, Storm, and I like your cousin Ian."

He glanced at her. They were sitting in the back of a cab on their way back to the hotel. It was dark, but the moonlight, as well as the bright lights from the buildings they passed, provided sufficient light for them to see each other's features clearly. But even if he hadn't been able to see her, he would have definitely been able to smell her. The perfume she was wearing was a luscious, blatantly sensual scent and it was doing downright crazy things to his libido.

"Yeah, and I could tell he liked you," he responded huskily. *Almost a little too much,* he thought. He smiled when he remembered the look on his cousin's face the moment he and Jayla had walked into the party. Ian's expression of appreciation was also shared by most of the other men present. His heart had swelled with pride that she was with him.

And he couldn't forget how Ian had pulled Jayla to him and planted a kiss on her lips when they'd been leaving. He grinned, knowing Ian had intended to give him a dose of his own medicine. Ian had wanted to get a rise out of him, the same way he enjoyed getting a rise out of his brothers whenever he kissed their wives. Now he knew how it felt.

"I can't wait to get to the hotel to get out of these shoes. They are killing my feet."

Storm smiled and was glad that because of the darkness, Jayla couldn't see the heated gleam in his eyes. He couldn't wait to get her back to the hotel to get her out of something else. The sight of her in that dress had nearly driven him mad all night. He couldn't wait to see just what she had or didn't have underneath it.

"Lift your feet into my lap and I'll be glad to give you some temporary relief," he murmured, wanting to touch her any way he could. She didn't waste time taking him up on his offer and she shifted her body to slide her legs across his lap. He knew there was no way she could not feel the hardness of his groin with her legs resting across his thighs.

He went about removing the silver stiletto heels and began massaging her feet. Her panty hose felt smooth and silky to his touch, and the thought that he'd never pampered another woman this way suddenly hit him. He tossed the thought from his mind as he continued to gently and methodically stroke her feet, thinking there was nothing like a great pair of legs and she had a pretty nice pair.

"Umm, I could get used to this. You have gifted hands, Storm."

He smiled. "Anything to make you happy." He thought about what he'd said and shook his head. He wondered what it would take to make a woman like her completely happy.

"We got back too soon," Jayla said, and he glanced out of the cab's window to see they had arrived back at the hotel. He strapped her shoes back on her feet and felt an immediate sense of loss when she pulled her legs out of his lap.

He glanced over at her, determined to remove that disappointment from her voice. He leaned over, pulled her against him and captured her lips. The taste of her was arousing…as if he needed to be aroused more than he already was. In minutes, he had her groaning and liked the sound of it.

"My room or yours?" he whispered softly against her lips.

She stared at his mouth a moment before answering in a voice that increased his heart rate another notch. "I've never been inside a man's hotel room before and since this trip to New Orleans has been a first for me in a lot of ways, let's go to your room tonight."

He kissed her again, devouring her soft lips and thinking he could definitely get used to this.

Jayla awoke when she heard the ringing of the telephone. A quick glance at the clock on the nightstand indicated it was the wake-up call she had ordered. She watched as Storm reached over, picked up the receiver and, without answering, hung it back up. He then met her gaze and for a moment she thought she saw a quick instant of regret in his eyes when he said, "I guess it's time."

"Yeah, it seems that way," she said softly, not wanting to get out of bed and get dressed, although she knew that she should. She needed to go to her room and pack. Her flight was scheduled to leave in a few hours and she had to make sure that she arrived at the airport on time.

Heat spread low in her belly when Storm continued to look at her. Whenever he looked at her, it did things to her. She would remember every moment of last night. She had entered his hotel room and he had closed the door behind them. She had walked into his embrace and the kiss they'd shared had been blazing and within seconds he had removed her dress and panty hose, leaving her wearing only a thong.

She would never forget the way he had looked at her, how he had swept her up into his arms and carried her over to the bed and made love to her as if pleasing her were the most important thing in his life. The lovemaking that they had shared had been simply amazing.

"Do you need help packing?" he asked, looking breath-takingly handsome, sleep-rumpled and delicious. He smiled as he braced himself up on one elbow and looked down at her. He reached out and gently touched the nipples of her breasts. They hardened with his touch and she felt a warmth begin to build between her legs.

She returned his smile, knowing if she were to take him up on his offer she would never finish packing. "Thanks for the offer, but I believe I can manage."

She felt her smile slowly fade away as reality set in. Although she did not regret any of the time she had spent with him, she knew it was about to end. There was no other way, and it would be for the best. She had to shift her focus away from Storm and back to the baby she wanted more than anything. As soon as she got home, she would schedule an appointment with the fertility clinic to get things started. A continuation of Storm in her life would only complicate things and she didn't do well with complications. Besides, she knew there was no Mr. Right for her, especially one by the name of Storm Westmoreland.

So why was it so hard for her to get out of his bed? And why did she want to make love to him again, one last time before she finally walked out the door?

"I enjoyed our time together, Jayla."

His words interrupted her thoughts and she met his gaze, studied his eyes. "I did, too, and still no regrets, right?"

He reached out and threaded his fingers through her hair. "No regrets. We're adults and we did what we wanted to do."

A smile curved her mouth. "Thank you Storm for showing me how great lovemaking can be."

He looked at her, countered her smile. "You're welcome."

"But life goes on," she decided to say when more than anything she wanted to kiss him.

He nodded. "Yes, life goes on, but it won't be easy. If I were to run into you anytime soon," he said, gently smoothing his fingertips across her cheek, "there's no way I'll see you and not think about that red dress and those killer high heels, not to mention the only thing you were wearing under that dress."

She chuckled. "Shocked you, huh?"

A huge smiled tipped one corner of his mouth. "Yeah, you shocked me. You also pleased me."

Storm decided that what he couldn't tell her was that she was unlike any woman he had ever known. She was someone who could laugh with him, tease him and talk to him just about anything. And the sex had been amazing and there was no way he could let her go without making love to her again. He needed this one last time to seal the memory of their time together into his mind forever.

Forever.

That was a word he had never included in his vocabulary, one he had never associated with a woman. He didn't do forever, and never thought about it. But he had to admit that with Jayla Cole, he thought of things he had never thought of before. And he was glad for the time they had spent together. He had learned things about her that he otherwise might not have known, such as her passion for strawberry cheesecake and how she volunteered her spare time at Emory University Hospital's Cancer Center.

"Storm, I need to get up, get dressed and leave."

He stared at her, feeling a sense of finality and a part of him felt a sense of loss he'd never experienced before and one he couldn't explain. And then, suddenly, he wanted her with an urgency he had never wanted her or any woman before. Blood rushed through his veins and he breathed in deeply.

"Storm…"

He looked at her and his breath stopped. He had to have her again, this one last time. He eased her beneath him the same moment that he lowered his head and captured her lips, tasting her, mating his tongue over and over with hers. She had stamped her mark on him and now he was going to make sure he stamped his on her.

For just a little while, he would make her *his*, and if he

lived a hundred years, there would be no regrets. What he would have were memories to last a lifetime.

And from the way she was returning his kiss he could tell she wanted those memories, too.

Six

"So, how was your trip to New Orleans?" Lisa Palmer asked as she sat back in her chair at Jayla's kitchen table.

Jayla looked up and met her best friend's curious stare. "It was fine. Why do you ask?"

"Because I've noticed that since you've been back, you haven't said much about it."

Jayla drew in a deep breath and wished she could ignore Lisa's curious scrutiny. It was just like Lisa to pick up on her reference about the trip. She knew that sooner or later she would have to come clean and tell her friend everything, including her planned trip to the fertility clinic.

"Umm, why do I get the feeling that you're not telling me something?"

Cupping her chin in her palm, Jayla forced a smile. "You're imagining things."

Lisa shook her head. "No, I don't think so." She gazed

at her thoughtfully, then said, "There's something different about you. You look more relaxed and well-rested which can only mean one thing."

Jayla swallowed, wondering if she really had a different look about her. "What?" she asked softly.

Lisa's lips tilted into a deep smile. "That you got plenty of rest this trip, which is a good thing that I didn't go with you. Had I gone I would have worn you out with endless shopping and—"

"I ran into someone."

Lisa lifted a brow. When seconds ticked off and Jayla didn't say anything else, Lisa scooted closer in her chair. "Okay, are you going to keep me in suspense or are you going to tell me?"

Jayla took a sip of her lemonade before responding. "I ran into Storm Westmoreland."

Lisa placed her glass of lemonade down on the table. "Storm Westmoreland? The Perfect Storm?"

Jayla chuckled. "Yes, that Storm."

Lisa stared at her for a moment as she recalled Jayla once telling her about the crush she'd had on Storm Westmoreland at sixteen. And, like most women in the Atlanta area, she also knew about his reputation as a womanizer, and that's what bothered her the most. "What was Storm Westmoreland doing in New Orleans?" she asked, having a feeling there was a lot more to the story.

Jayla chuckled again. "He was attending a conference."

"And…?"

Jayla was quiet for a moment. She knew Lisa had a thousand questions and decided she might as well tell her everything or else she would get grilled to death. "And we ran into each other and one thing led to another and we ended up having an affair."

She almost grinned when she saw Lisa's jaw drop. She then watched as Lisa picked up her glass and drained it as if it contained something stronger than lemonade.

Lisa then turned her full attention to her. "You're no longer a virgin?" she asked as if her mind were in shock.

Jayla did grin this time. "Nope."

Lisa then slumped back in her chair and pinned her with a look. Jayla was well aware of *that* look. It was a look that said you'd better tell me everything and start from the beginning.

"Like I said," Jayla said, before she was hammered with relentless questions, "Storm and I ran into each other, decided to spend time together and one thing led to another."

"Evidently."

Now it was Jayla who pinned Lisa with a look. "And don't expect me to tell you *everything* because there are some details you're better off not knowing." Her mind was suddenly filled with thoughts of everything she and Storm had done. They had made love so many times she had lost count, and each time had been better than the last.

What she held special was the first time and how, afterward, he had drawn her bath water, gently picked her up into his arms and carried her into the bathroom. But it was the last time they'd made love on the morning she'd left, that stood out in her mind more than the others.

With a loving tenderness that had almost brought tears to her eyes, he had used his hands and mouth to drive her over the edge, making her body burn out of control for him. And it was only when she was about to come apart in his arms did he fill her and begin moving back and forth inside her, combining tenderness with compelling need, and sending her escalating into a sharp, shattering orgasm that had taken her breath away and had left her sated, exhausted and spent. And as much as she'd tried to stay awake, she had drifted off to sleep. They both had. When they had awakened, she'd dressed quickly and returned to her room to pack.

He had gone to her room with her to help her pack and the last kiss he had given her before she had walked out of the hotel room door for the airport had been off-the-charts fantastic. She knew that if she never made love to another man, she would always remember having that time with Storm. It had been more than just good, mind-blowing sex. For three days, he had made her feel special, as if knowing he'd been her first had been extraordinary and he was still in awe of the gift she had given him.

"Jayla?"

She jumped when Lisa snapped a finger in front of her face. "What?"

"You haven't answered my question."

Jayla frowned. "What question?"

"Do you have any regrets?"

Jayla immediately shook her head. "No. Twenty-six years was long enough to be a virgin, but I'd never met a man I felt worthy of giving myself to until Storm."

Lisa raised a dark brow. "With Storm's reputation, you thought he was worthy?"

"Yes, because he didn't try to snowball me into doing it with him. In fact, at first he actually tried resisting my advances. I'm the one who came on to him. And he always behaved like a perfect gentleman, giving me choices and not assuming anything."

Lisa nodded, and then a curious glint shone in her dark eyes. "Is everything we've heard about him true?"

Jayla tried to ignore the heat that was settling between her legs when she thought about just how true it was. When it came to lovemaking, Storm Westmoreland was a practiced and skillful lover. She couldn't help but smile. "Yes, everything we've heard is true."

A silly smirk appeared on Lisa's face and she sat back in her chair. "Damn. Some women have all the luck," she said with envy. She then smiled. "So when will the two of you see each other again?"

Jayla tried to ignore the ache that suddenly settled around her heart, convincing herself it was only indigestion. "We won't be seeing each other again. What we shared was nothing more than a no-strings-attached affair, and since neither of us is into relationships, we decided that when we returned to Atlanta, he would continue to do his thing and I would continue to do mine."

Lisa lifted a brow. "You don't have a 'thing' to do. You basically live a boring life. All you do is go to work and come home, except for those days when you're volunteering at the cancer center."

Jayla knew what Lisa said was true, but in a few weeks all of that would change. She smiled. "Well, I want you to know that my life will no longer be boring. I've decided to take the first step in doing something I've wanted to do for a long time."

"Oh, and what's that?"

"Have a baby."

Jayla watched Lisa's expression. She looked as if someone had just pulled a chair out from under her. Lisa looked at her long and hard before finally saying something. "What do you mean, have a baby?"

"Just what I've said. You of all people know how much I love children."

Lisa shrugged. "Hey, I love them, too, but I'm not planning to have any until Mr. Right comes alone and I'm ready to settle down and get married."

Jayla raised her eyes to the ceiling. "Well, yeah, but for some of us there is no Mr. Right, so I've decided not to wait any longer."

Lisa was quiet for a moment as she pinned Jayla with that look again. "Tell me you didn't deliberately try and get pregnant by Storm Westmoreland."

Jayla couldn't help but laugh. Lisa's question was so ridiculous. Storm Westmoreland would be the last man she would want to father her child. He was too controlling. "Trust me, that thought never crossed my mind. Besides, I would never trick any man that way. I made all the necessary arrangements before I left for New Orleans, and I'm going to go to a fertility clinic and have the procedure done."

Lisa quickly held up her hand. "Time out. Back up. What are you talking about?"

Jayla smiled. The expression on Lisa's face was both endearing and maddening. They were as close as sisters and she knew her best friend well enough to know that she would not agree with her decision regarding the fertility clinic. But then, Lisa didn't have any problems finding a Mr. Right since she was already involved in a serious relationship with a wonderful guy. Added to that was the fact that Lisa came from a big family, so she didn't know the meaning of loneliness.

"I'm talking about my decision to have a baby. I've already done the preliminary paperwork and they'd located a potential donor who fits the profile I've requested. All that's left is for me to take another physical, which is scheduled for next Friday. Once it's determined when I'm most fertile during my cycle, I'll be going in to have the procedure done. If I'm not successfully inseminated on the first try, then there will be another try and if necessary, a third or however many times it takes. I'm sure my eggs will eventually be ripe for some donor's sperm," she said smiling.

Lisa, Jayla noticed, wasn't smiling back. In fact, she looked mortified. "Tell me you're joking about this, Jayla."

Jayla sighed deeply. She then worked her bottom lip between her teeth several times, which was something she tended to do when she was bothered by something. Over the years, Lisa may not have agreed with everything she did but had always supported her. Jayla knew because of her friend's traditional beliefs, this would be a hard sell, which was why she had put off telling Lisa about her plans.

She lifted her chin. "No, I'm not joking, Lisa. I've made up my mind about this. You may not agree with what I'm doing, but I really do need you to support me on this. I want a baby more than anything."

"But there are other options, Jayla."

"Yes, and I considered those other options and none will work for me. I want a baby not an involvement with a man who may not be Mr. Right, and I don't have time to wait until I finally get lucky. Times have changed. A woman no longer needs a man to get pregnant or to raise a child, and that's the way I want to do things."

Lisa didn't say anything for a long moment, then she reached across the table and captured Jayla's hand in hers. "Although I can understand some women having the procedure done in certain situations, your case is different, Jayla, and what you plan to do goes against everything I believe in. When it's possible, I think a child should benefit with the presence of both the mother and father in the home. But if you're hell-bent on going through with it, then I'll be there to do whatever you need me to do."

Jayla blinked back the tears in her eyes. "Thanks."

"Hey, Storm, get your mind back on the game, stop daydreaming and throw out a card."

Thorn Westmoreland's words recaptured Storm's attention and he threw out a card then leaned back in his chair and frowned. "I was not daydreaming and my mind *is* on the game," he said throwing out a card.

After another round of bid whist, Stone Westmoreland shook his head. "If your mind is on the game then you're a lousy card player since you just threw out a diamond instead of a heart which means you've reneged." A huge smile tilted the corners of Stone's lips. "But I'm not complaining since that puts me closer to winning."

Storm pushed back his chair and stood, glaring at his four brothers. Apparently they'd found his lack of concentration amusing but he didn't find a damn thing funny about it. "I'm sitting out for a while. I need some fresh air."

While he was walking away he heard his brother Thorn ask the others, "What's wrong with him?"

"Don't know," his brother Dare replied. "He's been acting strange ever since he got back from that conference in New Orleans."

"Maybe the pressures of being a fire captain is getting

to him," he heard his brother Chase add. "There's nothing worse than letting a job stress you out."

"Yeah," his other brothers agreed.

Storm shook his head when he opened the door and stepped out on the lanai. His brothers didn't know how wrong they were. His new promotion or work-related stress had nothing to do with the way he'd been acting since returning from New Orleans.

He glanced up and noticed a full moon and the stars in the sky. It was a beautiful night and he was glad he had come outside to appreciate the evening for a little while.

After Thorn and Tara had gotten married, they had moved into Tara's place since it was larger than Thorn's, but only temporarily. They were building their dream home on a parcel of the Westmoreland family homestead, which was located on the outskirts of town. It was a pretty nice area if you liked being out in the boon-docks and cherished your privacy.

Storm shook his head as an image of a woman forced its way into his head. It was the same image he'd been trying like hell to forget the past week. Jayla Cole.

He balled his hands into fists at his side as he wondered what was wrong with him. He'd had affairs before but none had affected him the way this one had. No woman had ever remained in his thoughts after the affair had ended. He'd known there would be memories, hell he had counted on savoring them. But he had wanted them safely tucked away until he was ready to revisit them. He hadn't counted on having no control of his own memories.

Visions of Jayla in the red dress were taking him to the cleaners and wringing him out. And then there were those images of the sway of her hips whenever she walked, whether she was in heels or flats. It didn't matter. The woman was sensuality on legs. She was a mouthwatering piece flat on her back as well. All he had to do was close his eyes and he was reliving the evenings filled with their mind-boggling, earth-shattering lovemaking.

She had fired up and completely satisfied a need within him that he hadn't known existed. Each and every time he had taken her to bed they had made incredible love. He could get her so wet, so hot, so ready, and likewise she could get him so hard, so needy, so out-of-his-mind greedy, to the point where getting inside her body was all he could think about; all he wanted.

And then there was the look on her face whenever she came. It was priceless. It was as if the force of what she felt stole her breath and the intensity of it exploded her world into tiny fragments as she tumbled into mindless completion. Seeing that experience on her face would then push him over the edge into the most potent climax he'd ever experienced; usually more than one—back to back.

"Damn," he let out a low growl and wiped a sheen of perspiration from his forehead with his hand. He was used to sexual experiences, but getting seduced by memories was something that he was not used to or comfortable with. Hell, he had even thought about dropping by her house to make sure she was all right. If that didn't beat all. He had never checked up on a woman after the affair ended.

"Storm, are you okay?"

He inhaled deeply when he heard his sister-in-law's voice and quickly decided that although it was dark, it wouldn't be a good idea for him to turn around just yet. There was a glow of light filtering out from the living room and he had gotten hard just thinking about Jayla.

"Storm?"

"Yeah, Tara, I'm fine." Seconds later when he was sure he had gotten his body back under control he turned around and smiled.

Tara Matthews was beautiful and had nearly blown Storm and his brothers away the first time they had seen her at their sister Delaney's apartment in Kentucky. And he might have even considered having a relationship with her, but he'd soon discovered that Tara was a handful. He and his brothers had quickly concluded that the only man who could possibly handle her was their brother Thorn, so they had deemed her Thorn's challenge. Now, a little more than two years later, she was Thorn's wife. But she still held a special place in his heart as well as the hearts of his brothers because in the end though Thorn may have handled her, Tara had proved that she was capable of handling Thorn, which wasn't an easy task.

He met her gaze and saw concern in her eyes. "I was worried about you," she said softly. "When I passed through the dining room and saw you missing, your brothers said you had needed fresh air. I didn't know if you were coming down with something, especially when they'd said you'd been playing badly tonight."

Storm laughed, then gave her a playful grin. "Hell, they claim I play lousy even when I'm winning."

Tara nodded smiling. "So, how was your trip to New Orleans?"

Funny you should ask, he thought as he slumped back against a column post. He sucked in a deep breath when another vision of Jayla floated through his mind. He envisioned his mouth finding her most sensitive areas, especially her ultra-hot spot and tilting her up to his mouth and making her scream.

"Storm?"

"Huh?"

"I asked how was your trip." She took a step closer to him and looked deeply into his eyes. "Are you sure you're okay, your eyes seemed somewhat dazed."

And my body is hard again but we won't go there, he thought, thinking the best thing to do was go back inside and play cards and hope that this time he could keep his mind on the game. "I'm fine and I had a great time in New Orleans. I even saw Ian while I was there and he mentioned that he would be in town for that charity benefit that you're working on."

A smile touched the corners of Tara's lips. "Really," she said excitedly. "That's the night we'll unveil the charity calendar for Kids' World and everyone will get to see Thorn as Mr. July."

Storm laughed. "I don't think that's the only reason Ian is coming, Tara," he said, thinking that maybe if he kept talking he wouldn't have to worry about visions of Jayla intruding. "The main reason Ian's coming is because you asked him to, but there's another reason."

Tara lifted her brow. "And what reason is that?"

A grin appeared on Storm's face. "He figures there will be a lot of pretty, single women in attendance."

Tara shook her head smiling, finally getting the picture. "Well, I'm sure there will be plenty of single women there since eleven of the men who posed for the calendar are still single. Thorn is the only one who has gotten married since those photos were taken."

Something suddenly pulled at Storm's memory. He remembered Jayla mentioning that she would be meeting Tara for lunch the Tuesday after returning to work. Unless those plans had changed, that meant the two of them would be meeting tomorrow. There was no way he could ask Tara about it without her wondering how he'd known. But if they were to meet tomorrow for lunch and if he knew where, he could unexpectedly drop by and pretend that he'd been in the area. For some reason he wanted to see Jayla again and if they *accidentally* ran into each other, she wouldn't think he had intentionally sought her out…although in essence, he would be doing just that.

"So, Tara, how about if I took you, Madison and Shelly to lunch tomorrow?" he suggested. He knew Dare's wife Shelly hadn't returned from visiting her parents in Florida, Stone's wife Madison would be leaving with Stone tomorrow on a book-signing trip to Kansas City, and if Tara had made other plans for lunch then he would find out soon enough.

"Thanks, Storm, that's really sweet of you, but Shelly and Madison will be out of town and besides I already have a lunch date. I'm meeting with a woman who's working with me on the charity benefit. Her company has agreed to pick up the tab for all the food and drinks that night."

Bingo. He was suddenly beginning to feel pretty good now. Confident. Cocky. Smug. He straightened from leaning against the post. "Oh, that's too bad. Where are you going?"

Tara lifted a brow. "Excuse me?"

He inhaled slowly, knowing he couldn't appear too inquisitive. The last thing he needed was for Tara to get suspicious of anything. "I asked where are you going for lunch? It might be a place where I've eaten before. Perhaps I can tell you whether the food and service are good."

Tara smiled. "Trust me, I know you've eaten at this

place plenty of times and can definitely vouch for the food and service being the best. My lunch date left it up to me to select a place and although I haven't told her yet, I'm going to suggest that we have lunch at Chase's Place."

His heart suddenly did a back flip and his mouth curved into a huge smile. Things couldn't have worked out better if he was planning things himself. Tara was taking Jayla to his brother's restaurant, a place where he ate lunch on a regular basis, so it wouldn't seem out of the ordinary if he showed up there tomorrow. "I think that's a wonderful choice."

She shook her head smiling and before she could say anything, Thorn's loud voice roared through the air. "Storm, get back in here if you're in this game, and you better not be out there kissing my wife."

Storm laughed. "He's a jealous kind of fellow, isn't he?" he asked, taking Tara's hand as they walked back inside

She grinned and he could see her entire face light up with absolute love for his brother. "Yes, but I wouldn't have him any other way."

"Chase's Place?" Jayla asked, making sure she had heard correctly.

"Yes," Tara said brightly on the other end of the phone. "It's a soul-food restaurant that's owned by my brother-in-law Chase Westmoreland, and the food there is wonderful."

Jayla rose from behind her desk, no longer able to sit. She knew the food there was wonderful but at the moment that wasn't what was bothering her. She recalled Storm saying that he routinely ate at his brother's restaurant. She was tempted to suggest they go someplace else but quickly remembered that she had been the one to suggest that Tara select the place for lunch. She sighed deeply. "I've eaten there before and you're right the food is wonderful."

"And he's promised to take good care of us."

Jayla raised a dark brow. "Who?" She heard Tara chuckle on the other end before answering.

"Chase. He's good at taking care of people. "

"Oh." It was on the tip of Jayla's tongue to say it must run in the family because Chase wasn't the only West-moreland who was good at taking care of people. She viv-idly remembered the way Storm had taken care of her, fulfilling and satisfying her every need.

She tried forcing the memories to the back of her mind. "What time do you want us to meet?"

"What about around one-thirty? That way the noonday lunch crowd won't bombard us. But if you think you'll be hungry before then we can—"

"No, one-thirty is fine and I'll meet you there." After ending the call, Jayla sat back at her desk. If she saw Storm again, what was the correct protocol to handle the situa-tion? Women and men had affairs all the time and she was sure that at some point they ran into each other again. Did they act casually as if nothing had ever happened between them and they were meeting for the first time? Or were they savvy enough to accept that they had shared something in-timate with no regrets, moved on and didn't make a big deal about it? She decided the latter would work. It wasn't as if they had been total strangers.

She glanced at her watch. One-thirty was less than five hours away. Although Atlanta was a big town, she and Storm were bound to run into each other soon or later, but part of her had been hoping it was later. She had expected to see him at the charity benefit, but had figured she would be prepared to see him by then. It was more than a week since they had been together, nine days, if you were counting, and unfortunately, she was.

She closed her eyes and exhaled a deep breath. If she saw him, she would play it cool, take the savvy approach and hope and pray that it worked.

"Is there a reason why you're hanging around here?"

Storm shrugged and shot his twin a beguiling smile. "I like this place."

The expression he read on Chase's face said he knew better, since he only dropped by to eat and rarely hung around to socialize. He usually was too busy pursuing women to visit with his brother for very long. His answering machine had maxed out while he'd been out of town and his phone hadn't stopped ringing since he'd been back. But for some reason, he wasn't interested in returning any of those women's calls.

"Well, if you don't have anything better to do with your time, how about waiting tables?" Chase said, interrupting his thoughts. "One of my waitresses called in sick and we're shorthanded."

Storm glanced at his watch while shaking his head. "Sorry. I like you, Chase, but not that much." He turned and glanced at the entrance to his brother's restaurant and wondered if perhaps Tara and Jayla had changed their minds and decided to go someplace else since it was past lunchtime. No sooner had that possibility crossed his mind, than the door swung open and the two women entered.

His breath caught at the sight of Jayla. Because he was sitting at the far end of the counter, he knew she wouldn't be able to see him but he could definitely see her. She was dressed differently than she'd been in New Orleans. Today, Jayla was Miss Professional in her chic navy blue power suit. She still looked stunning and as sexy as sin. Storm could feel his libido going bonkers. He swung around to Chase. "Hey, I've changed my mind. I will help you out after all."

Chase raised a suspicious brow. "Why the change of heart?"

"Because if a man can't depend on his twin brother in a time of need, then who can he depend on?" Storm asked, giving Chase a boyish grin.

Chase cast a speculative glance over Storm's shoulder and said dryly, "I hope the person you're all fired up at seeing is the woman with Tara and *not* Tara. I would hate for Thorn to kill you."

Storm chuckled. "Relax. I got over Tara a long time ago. I just like getting a rise out of Thorn."

He leaned over the counter and snagged a pencil from Chase's shirt pocket and tucked it behind his ear. He then picked up a pad off the counter. "Who's working the table where they're sitting?"

"Pam."

Storm smiled. "Then tell Pam to take a break or, better yet, tell her to find another table to work. I got that one covered." Before Chase could say anything, Storm stood and headed over to where Tara and Jayla were sitting.

"We made perfect timing," Tara said smiling. "Had we arrived any earlier this place would have been packed." The menus were in a rack on the table and she passed one to Jayla.

Jayla nodded as she opened the menu. She was tempted to glance around but decided not to. Chances were if Storm had been there earlier as a part of the lunch crowd he would have already left.

After they had looked over the menus for a few moments, Tara glanced up, smiled and asked, "So what are you going to get?"

Tara's question recaptured her attention and she couldn't help but return the other woman's smile. Already she'd decided that she liked Tara Westmoreland. They had spoken several times on the phone, but this was the first time they had actually met in person. Jayla thought the woman was simply gorgeous and could quickly see how she had captured the heart of motorcycle tycoon, Thorn Westmoreland.

"Umm," Jayla said smiling as if in deep thought as she glanced back down at the menu and licked her lips. "Everything looks delicious, but I think I'll get—"

"Good afternoon, ladies, what can I get you?"

Jayla's head snapped up and she blinked upon seeing Storm standing beside their table. "Storm!" Without thinking, she said his name as intense heat settled deep in her stomach.

Storm's mouth curved into a devilish grin, and that grin reminded her of sensations he could easily elicit, tempting her into partaking in any number of passionate indulgences. "I'm not on the menu, Jayla, but if I'm what you want, I can definitely make an exception."

Seven

"**I** take it the two of you know each other," Tara said curiously as a smile touched her lips. She glanced from Storm to Jayla.

Jayla cleared her throat, wondering how much she should say. Before she could decide on how to respond, Storm spoke up.

"Jayla's father was my first fire captain and was like a second father to me," he said, giving them his killer-watt smile. "So, yes, we know each other."

Jayla swallowed deeply, grateful for Storm's timely and acceptable explanation.

"It's good seeing you again, Jayla."

She smiled. "It's good seeing you, too," she said, meaning every word, although she wished that she didn't.

"And you look good, by the way."

Her smile widened. "Thanks." He looked rather good, too, she thought. He was dressed in a pair of khaki trousers and a polo shirt. And he smelled good. His cologne could always jump-start her senses. It was a good thing she was already sitting down because she could actually feel her knees weaken. Everything about Storm was a total turn-on—the rippling muscles beneath his shirt, his extraordinary butt, long legs, his too-hot grin and eyes so dark they reminded you of chocolate chips…. Had she forgotten that she had a weakness for chocolate chips just as bad as her weakness for strawberry cheesecake?

She glanced over at Tara and saw that she was still watching them and Jayla decided it wouldn't be a bad idea to go ahead and place her order. She cleared her throat. "I'll have today's special with a glass of iced tea."

"All right." Storm scribbled down Jayla's order, not knowing and not really caring what today's special was. The only thing on his mind was that he was getting the chance to see her again.

He then turned his attention to Tara and smiled. "And what will you have Mrs. Westmoreland?"

Tara lifted a brow. "An explanation as to why you're waiting on tables."

Storm chuckled. He was busted. Leave it to Tara to ask questions. She'd been hanging around his brother Thorn too long. "Chase was shorthanded so I thought I'd pitch in and help him out."

Tara nodded, but the look she gave let him indicated that she knew there was more to the story than that. He wondered if parts of their conversation last night were coming back to her. "That was kind of you, Storm, and I'll have today's special, as well, with a glass of lemonade."

Storm wrote down her order, then said, "I'll go ahead and bring your drinks." He winked at them and then walked off.

Jayla watched him walk away. When she returned her attention back to Tara she knew the woman had been watching her watch Storm. "Small world, isn't it?" she asked trying to pull herself together before she actually started drooling.

Tara smiled. "Yes, it is a small world," she agreed as she studied Jayla. Storm had been blatantly flirting with the woman, which was nothing surprising. Tara had seen Storm in action many times before. But something was different with the way he had flirted with Jayla; however, at the moment she couldn't put a finger on just what that difference was.

"I'm looking forward to the charity benefit," Jayla was saying, rousing Tara from her musings and reminding her of the reason for their meeting.

"So am I, and the committee appreciates Sala Industries agreeing to be our food and beverage sponsor. Kids' World will benefit greatly from their contribution. The money raised from the calendar will be more than enough to make the children's dreams come true."

Jayla smiled in agreement. "Doesn't it bother you that your husband is Mr. July on that calendar?"

Tara laughed as she remembered how she'd maneuvered Thorn into posing for the calendar. Actually, they had come to an agreement only after Thorn had made her an offer she couldn't refuse. "No, I'm not bothered at all. It will be nice knowing other women will find my husband as sexy as I do."

Jayla nodded. She had seen Thorn Westmoreland before in person and the man was definitely sexy. But she didn't think anyone was sexier than Storm. She couldn't help but glance to where he had gone. He was behind the counter preparing their drinks and, as if he knew she was looking at him, he lifted his head, met her gaze and smiled.

It was a smile that sent shivers all the way through her body. It was also a smile that seemed to say, *I remember everything about those days in New Orleans.* She couldn't help returning his smile as she also remembered everything about their time together.

When she turned her attention back to Tara, Jayla realized that Tara had noticed the silent exchange between her and Storm. "Umm…I, well—" she started to say, feeling somewhat embarrassed that Tara had caught her ogling Storm.

Tara reached across the table and touched her hand. "No need to explain, Jayla. I'm married to a Westmoreland so I understand."

Jayla pulled in a deep breath, wondering how could Tara possibly understand when she didn't understand her feelings for Storm. "It's nothing but simple chemistry," she decided to say to explain.

Tara smiled, thinking of her reaction to Thorn Westmoreland the first time she had seen him. "Happens to the best of us, trust me."

Jayla laughed, suddenly feeling relaxed and thinking that, yes, she really did like Tara Westmoreland.

Chase shook his head as he stared at his brother. "Are you going to stand there all day and stare at that woman with Tara?"

Storm met Chase's gaze and grinned. "I like watching her eat. I love the way her mouth moves."

Chase's gaze followed Storm and he didn't see anything fascinating about the way she was eating, although he would be the first to admit that she was good-looking. He turned his attention back to Storm. "Who is she?"

"Adam's daughter."

Chase snapped his gaze back to the table where Tara and the woman were sitting. "Are you saying that's Adam Cole's girl, all grown up?"

"Yes."

"Wow. I haven't seen her since she was in high school. He would bring her in here every once and a while for dinner." He let out a low whistle. "Boy, has she changed. She was a cute kid, but now she is definitely a looker. I'd say she is a woman who looks ripe for loving."

Storm turned and glared at his brother as he leaned against the counter and shoved his hands deep into his pants pockets. "I'm going to ignore the fact that you said that."

Chase smiled. "Hey, man, I didn't know things were *that* way with her," he offered by way of apology.

Storm's glare deepened. "And what do you perceive as *that* way?"

Chase's smile widened. Storm was so used to getting a rise out of people that he couldn't recognize when someone was trying to get a rise out of him. "You're interested in her. *That's* obvious."

Storm shrugged. "Of course I'm interested in her. Adam was someone I cared a lot about. He was like a second father to me. He was—"

"We're not talking about Adam, Storm. We're talking about his daughter. Come on and admit it. You're interested in her as a woman and not as Adam's daughter."

Storm frowned. "I'm not going to admit anything."

Chase chuckled. "Then why did you get jealous a few minutes ago?"

Storm blinked, then looked at his twin as if he were stone crazy, definitely had gone off the deep end. "Jealous?" he repeated, wondering how Chase could think such a thing. "The word *jealous* is not in my vocabulary."

Chase studied his brother's face and knew he had pushed him enough for one day, but couldn't resist taking one final dig. "Then it must have been added rather recently. Not only is it now in your vocabulary, you should spell the word with a capital *J*. And I thought the reason you were acting strange had to do with work. The way I see it, that woman sitting over there definitely has her hook in and is reeling you in."

Storm drew in a deep breath, squared his shoulders. The eyes that stared at his twin were hard, ice cold. "You're going to regret the day you said that."

Chase laughed. "And I have a feeling that you're going to regret the day you didn't figure it out for yourself."

Jayla slipped off her pumps as soon as she walked into the house and closed the door behind her. She let out a deep breath. Lunch with Tara Westmoreland had gone well and they had finalized a lot of items for the charity benefit. But what stood out in her mind more than anything was seeing Storm again.

More than once she had glanced his way. The heat in his eyes had ignited a slow, sensual burn within her. Across the distance of the room, he had silently yet expertly aroused her, almost making concentration on her discussion with Tara impossible.

And when he had placed their meals on the table, her

eyes had been drawn to his hands and it didn't take much to remember how skilled his fingers were, and how those fingers had known just the right places on her body to touch to drive her crazy. It was only when he had left the restaurant, shortly after serving their lunch, that her mind had become functional. Only then had she been able to zero in on the business that she and Tara had needed to accomplish.

On her drive back to the office, she had to remind herself several times that there was nothing between her and Storm and that any future involvement with him was out of the question. They each had a different agenda. To consider a possible relationship between them would only complicate things. What they had shared in New Orleans, just great sex, was over.

Placing her purse on the counter that separated the kitchen from her dining room, she started sorting through the mail she had retrieved from her mailbox and smiled when she saw a letter from the fertility clinic.

Tearing it open, she quickly scanned the contents and her smile widened. It was a letter reminding her of the physical that was scheduled for the next week and information about the insemination procedure.

Placing the letter in the drawer, she laughed, feeling elated, happy beyond words. She anxiously awaited that day—after the procedure was done—when a doctor would confirm she was pregnant. Although Lisa didn't totally agreed with what she planned to do, at least her friend would be there to support her. And, of course, Lisa had agreed to be her child's godmother.

In her heart, Jayla believed things would work out. She had a good friend who would stand by her and she had a good job. And as she had told Lisa, if the artificial insemination didn't work the first time around, she would try a second and, if need be, a third time. She would repeat the procedure as many times as it took to get pregnant whatever the cost. Thanks to the trust fund her father had left for her, as well as the insurance funds that had been left after all the burial expenses had been taken care of, she could afford making her dream of having a baby come true.

She decided to take a shower and relax before fixing dinner. Later, she would find a comfortable spot on her sofa to sit and prop her feet up on her coffee table and enjoy a good book. She tried shaking off the lonely feeling that she suddenly felt. Lisa had a date with her boyfriend Andrew tonight, which meant she wasn't available for a chat.

She tried not to recall that this time nearly a week and a half ago, she had been in New Orleans with Storm. Nor did she want to think about how much she had enjoyed his company. Of course, the time they had spent in bed had been great, but there had been more than that. She had discovered a fun side to Storm. Before New Orleans, she'd always assumed that he was a really serious sort of guy.

She had enjoyed laughing with him, talking to him, dancing with him, sharing food with him and going sight-seeing with him. He had been full of surprises in more ways than one. She couldn't help but compare him to the last guy she had dated, Erik Turner. Erik had turned out to be an A-number-one bore and had expected they'd go straight to her bedroom when he'd brought her home from their first date. He had actually gotten pissed off when she'd turned him down.

Frowning, she headed for her bedroom as she remembered how angry she had gotten, too, that night. Angry for having such high expectations that most men would treat a woman like a lady, decently respectable and not assume anything—especially on the first date. Erik had been included in a long line of disappointments for her, but he had definitely been the last straw and had been an eye-opener. That night Jayla realized that she didn't want to be one of those women who were in such a frenzy to be involved in a relationship that they failed to look at the signs that said, "This may not be the best person for me."

Another pitfall she had avoided, which was the main reason she had remained a virgin for so long, was the mistake some women made of equating sex with love. She'd learned from listening to the women she worked with, that some women still believed that if a man slept with her, it meant he loved her. She definitely hadn't assumed such a thing with her and Storm. It had been her hormones and not her heart that had been raging out of control. Storm didn't love her and she didn't love him. She hadn't expected anything from him and he hadn't expected anything from her. They had communicated well both in and out of bed, and the one thing they understood and agreed upon was that their affair would be one that led nowhere.

Sighing, she began removing her clothes for her shower. But as much as she didn't want to think about it, she couldn't get the memory of Storm and the way he had looked at her today out of her mind.

Drawing in a deep breath, Storm raised his hand to knock, then pulled back as he asked himself, for the umpteenth time, why he was standing in front of Jayla's front door. And no matter how many times he asked the question, the answer always came up the same.

He still wanted her.

Seeing her today had done more harm than good and what Chase had said hadn't helped matters. The notion that Jayla had hooked him was preposterous. Okay, he would admit she was still in his system. He had discovered that a man didn't have sex with a woman at the magnitude that he'd had with Jayla and not have some lingering effects. Lingering effects he could handle; the notion of some woman reeling him in, he could not.

Tonight, and only tonight, he would break his rule of not performing repeats after an affair ended. But he had to make sure that the only thing that was pulling him back to her was the incredible sex they'd shared. Physical he could handle, but anything that bordered on emotional he could not.

Taking another deep breath, he finally raised his hand and knocked on the door. As he waited for her to answer it, he hoped to God that he wasn't making a huge mistake.

He was about to knock again when he heard the sound of her voice on the other side. "Who is it?"

"It's me, Jayla. Storm."

She slowly opened the door and the anticipation of the removal of the solid piece of wood that stood between them sent a shiver of desire up his spine and down to his midsection. When she opened the door enough for him to see her, the sight of her nearly knocked him to his knees like a gale-force wind. It was obvious that she had just gotten out of the shower. Her hair was loose, flowing around her shoulders, and there were certain parts of her, not covered by her short bathrobe, that were still wet. He itched to take the robe off her to see what, if anything, she was wearing underneath it.

"Storm, what are you doing here?"

Her voice, low in pitch yet high in sensuality, rapidly

joined forces with desire that had already taken over his body. He was almost afraid to stand there and look at her. Too much longer and he might be driven to topple her to the floor and make love to her then and there.

"Storm?"

Claiming that he just happened to be in the neighborhood would sound pretty lame when she lived in North Atlanta and he resided in the southern part of town. Believing that honesty was the best policy, he decided to tell her the truth as his gaze locked on hers. "Seeing you today made me realize something," he murmured softly as he leaned in her doorway.

He watched her throat move when she swallowed. "What?"

"That I didn't get enough of you in New Orleans. I want you again."

He heard her inhale sharply and the sound triggered the memory of how her voice would catch just seconds before she came. His mind was remembering and his body was, too. He was tempted to pull her close and let her feel just how hard she was making him. "May I come in?" he decided to ask when she didn't say anything.

"Storm…"

"I know I shouldn't have come and I'm just as confused about showing up here as you are," he quickly said. "But seeing you today *really* did do something to me, Jayla, and it's something that's never happened to me before. It was as if my body went on overload and you're the only person who can shut it down. Since returning from New Orleans, I've been constantly reminded of the best sex I've ever had, and tonight I couldn't handle things any longer."

He sighed deeply. There. He'd said it. He'd been honest and upfront with her, although it had nearly killed him to admit such a thing. Even to his ears his predicament sounded almost like an addiction. His blood was pumped up a notch. Every muscle in his body ached at the thought of making love to her again and a part of him knew the look in his eyes was just shy of pleading. He might even go so far as to follow the Temptations' lead and sing out loud, "Ain't Too Proud To Beg."

It was all rather pathetic, but at the moment there wasn't a damn thing he could do about it. Jayla Cole was under his skin…at least temporarily. Just one more time with her should obliterate this madness. At least, that's what he hoped.

He watched her as she tried to make up her mind about him, but patience had never been one of his strong points and he couldn't help asking, "So are you going to let me in?"

Silence filled the air.

Moments later, Jayla sighed deeply. Her mind was in battle over what she *should* do versus what she *wanted* to do. She knew what she should do was send Storm packing after reminding him of their agreement. But what she really wanted to do was give him what she knew they both desired.

Just one more time, she decided. What could possibly be wrong in giving in to an indulgence just one more time? However, more than just once would be a complication she didn't need. Her heart hammered hard in her chest. She knew once he stepped inside and closed the door behind him, that would be the end of it…or the beginning. But as her body began to slowly tremble, her control began slipping. She knew that tonight she needed him just as much as he seemed to need her. He was right. This *was* madness.

"Yes," she finally said, taking a step back. "You can come in."

He entered and closed the door behind him. Locked it. The click sounded rather loud in the now awkward silence between them. That small sound was enough to push her heart into overdrive, making it beat that much faster.

"Thirsty?" she asked, deciding she should at least offer him a drink.

"Yes, very."

She turned toward the kitchen and was surprised when he reached out, gently grabbed her, pulled her close to him and wrapped his arms around her. "This is what I'm thirsty for, Jayla. The taste of you."

When her lips opened on a breathless sigh, his tongue swept into her mouth as if he needed to taste her as much as he needed to breathe. His lips were hot and demanding, and his tongue was making love to her mouth with an intensity that overwhelmed her. Helpless to do anything else, she looped her arms around his neck and held on while the heat of him consumed her, breaching any barrier and snatching away any resistance she might have had.

Too late. He was inside and intended to fill her to capacity in more ways than one.

She pushed good judgment, initial misgivings and any lingering doubts aside. She would deal with them later. Right now, being in Storm's arms this way was most important and demanded her full concentration. And everything about him—his scent, his strength, his very sensuality—permeated her skin, seeped into her blood and sent her senses spinning.

When he tore his mouth away from hers, she drew in a long audible sigh. She looked up at him and the air surrounding them seemed to crackle with ardent awareness. He reached out and traced a slow path down the center of her neck, then slowly pushed aside her robe to reveal what was underneath.

Nothing.

She heard his sharp intake of breath and he pushed the robe off her shoulders to the floor. "A few moments ago, I was thirsty for your mouth, but now I'm starving for this," he said reaching out and stroking her between the legs. "Once I get you in bed, I plan to make love to you all night."

His voice was low, uneven and so sexy that it sent shock waves all through her body. She met his gaze, saw the deep darkening of his eyes and any grip she had on reality slipped, joining her robe on the floor.

"That's a promise I intend to hold you to, Storm Westmoreland," she said on a breathless sigh, just seconds before he swept her into his arms.

Eight

"Which way to your bedroom?"

"Straight ahead and to your right."

Storm didn't waste any time taking her there and immediately placed her naked body in the middle of the bed. He took a step back to look at her. For a moment, he couldn't move, too overwhelmed by her beauty to do anything but to take it all in…and breathe. He ached to make love to her, and sink his body into the wet warmth of hers.

Love her.

Air suddenly left his lungs in a whoosh and he summoned all the strength he could not to fall flat on his face. The thought that he wanted to love her had been unintentional, absolutely ridiculous, outlandish and totally absurd. He only did non-demanding relationships and short-term affairs. He wasn't into strings, especially the attached kind.

He suddenly felt a tightening in his chest at the same time that he felt a bizarre quickening around his heart.

Hell! Something was wrong with him. Then, on second thought, maybe nothing was wrong with him. He was merely imagining things. He was aching so badly to be with Jayla again that he wasn't thinking straight. That had to be it. When he got home later tonight, on familiar turf, his mind would be clear. And spending a day at the station tomorrow around the guys would definitely screw his head back on straight.

"Are you going to stand there all night, Storm?"

He blinked, attempting to clear his mind and immediately became entranced with the warmness of Jayla's smile and the teasing heat of intimacy in her eyes. He swallowed deeply and tried to get a grip, but all he got was a harder arousal. "Not if I can help it," he said, suddenly needing to connect with her that instant. He needed to touch her, taste her, mate with her.

Right now.

He yanked his T-shirt over his head and then began fumbling with the fastening of his jeans, and became irritated when the zipper wouldn't slide down fast enough because of the size of his erection. Finally, he was able to tug his jeans down his legs and quickly stepped out of them. He reached down and took a condom packet out of the back pocket of the now discarded garment.

After he took the necessary steps, he looked at her and one corner of his mouth quirked up. "Now to keep that promise."

Simply looking at Storm caused Jayla's blood to pump rapidly through her veins. The look in his eyes said that he would hold nothing back. Her pulse quickened as he slid his body onto the bed. He moved, with the grace of a leopard, the prowl of a tiger and the intent of a man who wanted a woman. Overhead, the glow from the ceiling light magnified the broad expanse of his chest. He was perfectly built, his flesh a chocolate brown and every muscle well defined.

When he joined her on the bed she couldn't stop herself from reaching out to touch him. Her fingers trembled as she ran them through the dark, tight curls on his chest, and she smiled when she heard his breathing hitch. Hers did likewise when she felt the hardness of him press against her thigh. Her gaze was drawn to his nipples. They were hard, erect, and she wanted to know the texture of them under her tongue. He had tasted her breasts many times, but she'd never tasted his.

Leaning forward, her mouth opened over a stiff bud and her tongue began sliding around it, tasting it, absorbing it, sucking it. But for her, that wasn't enough. Reaching down she took hold of his hard heated flesh and her thumb and forefingers began caressing the hot tip. This was the first time she had ever tried to bring a man pleasure, to drive him insanely wild with desire with her hands. And from the sounds Storm was making, it seemed she was doing a good job.

When she heard him groan her name, the sound forced from deep within his throat, she lifted her head, but continued to let her hand clutch him, caress him, stroke him. "Umm?" she responded as she moved her mouth upward to take a tiny bite of his neck, branding him.

"You've pushed me too far, Jayla," Storm growled, as the need within him exploded. With one quick flick of his wrist, he tumbled her backward, ignoring her squeal of surprise. But she didn't resist and instead of moving from him, she moved to him, reaching up and looping her arms around his neck as he placed his body over hers, pressing his erection against the heat of her feminine core.

"Gotta get inside," he whispered brokenly as his hand clutched her waist, his thighs held hers in place. Taking her arms from around his neck, he captured her wrists and placed them above her head. He looked down at her, met her gaze at the same time he pushed himself inside of her.

He gasped. The pleasure of being inside of her was almost too much. He tipped his head back and roared an animalistic sound that mirrored the raging need within him. Then he began moving, in and out, straining his muscles, flexing his pelvis, rolling his hips while holding her in a firm grip, rocking her world, just mere seconds away from tumbling his own.

The bed started to shake and the windows seemed to rattle, but the only storm that was raging out of control was him, pelting down torrents of pleasure instead of sheets of rain. He didn't flinch when he felt her fingernails dig deeper into her flesh, but he did groan when he felt her inner muscles squeeze him, clench him, milk him. The woman was becoming a pro at knowing just what it took to splinter his mind and make him explode. No sooner had he thought the word, he felt her body do just that.

"Storm!"

And while she toppled over into oblivion, he continued to move in and out, claiming her as his.

His.

The thought of her belonging to him, and only to him, pushed him over the edge in a way he had never been pushed before. He thrust deep into her body, burying himself to the hilt, as his own release claimed him, ripped into him—not once, not twice, not even three times. The ongoing sensations that were taking over his body were more than he could stand.

"Jayla!"

And she was right there with him, lifting her hips off the bed, opening wider for him, moving with him, as they drove each other higher and higher on waves of excruciating pleasure.

The first light of dawn began slipping into the windows, fanning across the two naked bodies in bed. Jayla slowly awoke and took a long, deep breath of Storm and the lingering scent of their lovemaking.

It was there, in the air, the scent of her, of them—raw, primitive—the aftermath of her crying out in ecstasy, clutching his shoulders, pushing up her hips while he drove relentlessly into her, going as far as he could go, then tumbling them both over the edge as their releases came simultaneously.

She closed her eyes as panic seized her. What on earth had she done? All she had to do was open her eyes and glance over at Storm who was lying on his side facing her, still sleeping with a contented look on his face, to know what she had done. What she needed to really ask herself was how had it happened and why.

Storm had a reputation of not being a man who looked up a woman for a second helping. Once an affair ended, it was over. If that was the case, then why had he dropped by? What was there about her that had made him come back for more?

Jayla's features slipped into a frown. Although most

women would have been ecstatic that Storm had deemed them special enough to grace their bed a second time, to her he was a distraction. And a distraction was the last thing she needed now, especially with her upcoming appointment at the fertility clinic. If he were to find out about her plans, like Lisa he would probably try and talk her out of it. But unlike Lisa, he wouldn't understand her decision, or support her anyway, even if he disagreed with her.

She took a quick glance at him and wondered why it mattered to her that he might not support what she planned to do? Jayla was pretty sure Storm would frown upon the idea of her having a baby by artificial insemination. Like her father, Storm was a traditionalist. He believed in doing things the old-fashioned way. She had to admit that at least in the bedroom she found Storm's old-fashioned, always-remain-a-gentleman ways endearing. Being a gentleman didn't mean he wouldn't engage in some off-the-charts, blow-your-mind hot sex like they had definitely shared last night. It simply meant that he would never try anything that made her feel uncomfortable. Nor would he ever assume anything. The only reason he was still in her bed at the crack of dawn was because he had asked if it was okay for him to stay the night. He hadn't just assumed that it was. If only she could shake his belief that a woman could not manage both a career and motherhood. How primitive was it for someone to think that way in this day and time?

She shook her head as she quietly slipped out of bed thinking Storm had definitely earned his rest. The man had energy that she wished she could bottle. No sooner had they completed one climax, he was going down for another, and somehow he always managed to take her with him. It was as if his orgasms—and the man had plenty—always triggered hers. Multiple orgasms were something she'd read about and at the time, the thought of it happening to anyone seemed too far-fetched to consider. But she was living witness that it was possible. She smiled thinking Storm had spoiled her. She wouldn't know how to act if another man ever made love to her.

Her smile slowly died at the thought of making love to another man. Would she spend the rest of her life comparing every future lover to The Perfect Storm? She shook her head as she made her way into the bathroom for a shower. She was getting in deeper by the minute.

Storm woke slowly to the sound of running water and the scent of jasmine. He smiled, closing his eyes again as visions of what he and Jayla had done played through his mind like a finely tuned piano.

He reopened his eyes, thinking he was just as confused now as he'd been the night before. He wasn't sure why he was here in Jayla's bed instead of his own bed. Then he remembered. He'd had to be with her last night. He had been willing to say or do anything to get back into her bed. Even if it had meant begging.

He glanced at the clock on her nightstand. It was early, but time for him to go. He had to report to the station today to pull a twenty-four hour shift. He thoroughly enjoyed his new position of fire captain. To move from the ranks of lieutenant had meant many nights and weekends of studying for the fire department's promotional exam. During that time, he had given up a lot of things, including women. And even then, the thought of going without one hadn't bothered him. There hadn't been one single woman that he could name that he had missed making love to during all that time.

He closed his eyes again, not ready to move, not sure that he could if he wanted to. But the thought of Jayla, naked, wet and standing beneath a shower of water suddenly made him go hard, as if his body could do anything else around her.

He sighed deeply and suddenly the features of that old woman, the one who had read his palm in New Orleans, flitted across his mind at the same time the words she had spoken rang through his ears: *You are about to make unexpected changes in your life and although you yearn for peace, turbulence is in your future. Keep your sights high, be patient and let destiny take its course.*

He opened his eyes, quickly sat up and glanced around the room. It was as if the old woman's voice were right there. He shook his head, thinking he was definitely losing it.

He turned when he heard the sound of a door opening and glanced over his shoulder to see Jayla walk out of the bathroom with a towel wrapped tightly around her. She gave him a soft smile that immediately made him go hard…as if he wasn't already. And no matter how much he thought he was crazy this morning, he didn't have one single regret about last night.

"You should have woken me up and I would have joined you in the shower," he said standing, and crossing the room to her.

He watched as her gaze took in his nakedness, as it left his face to slowly roam down his chest, down past his stomach to settle…yeah, right there. He felt his erection get larger, become harder and saw her eyes grow dark with desire and her cheeks become flushed.

"You like being in your natural state, don't you?" she asked, lifting her gaze back to his.

He smiled. "Yes, and I like you being in your natural state, too."

She shook her head and chuckled. "I think we need to talk."

"I'd rather do something else." His smile widened. All she had to do was to drop her gaze back to his midsection to know what he had in mind.

She cleared her throat. "Well, unfortunately we both have jobs to go to this morning, right?"

"You would have to remind me of that, wouldn't you?" he asked, pulling her into his arms. "Have dinner with me at Anthony's tomorrow night."

She quickly pulled back. "Dinner?"

He dipped his head and captured an earlobe in his mouth. He'd heard the surprise in her voice. Hell, he was even surprised that he had suggested such a thing. "Yes, dinner. We can talk then, okay?" He knew what she wanted to talk about. She wanted to know why he was not adhering to their agreement. He hoped when he saw her again he would have some answers.

"Storm…I don't think that we—"

He lifted her chin with the tip of his finger so their eyes could meet. "Like you said, we need to talk, Jayla, and we can't do it here or at my place."

She nodded, understanding. At least at Anthony's, there wouldn't be any bedrooms around. "Okay."

Then Storm captured Jayla's mouth in a kiss that he definitely needed. The taste of her was like a drug to which he was addicted. She was a problem that needed a solution, but for now…

* * *

Wednesdays had always been referred to as over-the-hump day and it wasn't until today that Jayla actually understood what it meant…at least in terms of her and Storm.

It was almost lunchtime and Jayla was still besieged with constant memories of the night she'd spent with Storm. She glanced around to make sure no one noticed the blush that had to have appeared on her face, even with her dark skin tone.

She was in a room with, of all people, the vice president of the company, as well as the sales and advertising managers for Sala Industries. It was that time of the year when she needed to prepare the annual public relations report that the company distributed to the general public, interest groups and stockholders to make everyone aware of the company's activities and accomplishments the previous year. One of Sala's main goals for the year had been to increase their involvement in community affairs. Being a part of the charity benefit for Kids' World was one of the many projects they had undertaken to do just that.

Jayla had worked for the company since college and up until recently, the job had been the single most important thing in her life outside of her relationship with her father. After his death, she had moved her job up to the number one spot, which was why she had made a decision to have a baby. She had needed a life outside of work and someone to share that life with her. She smiled, thinking that she had only eight days to go before she went to the fertility clinic for her physical, the first step toward making her dream come true.

She glanced across the conference table and saw Lisa looking at her strangely. She lifted a brow and Lisa surreptitiously lifted one back. Jayla couldn't help but smile. Evidently, Lisa had seen her blush a few times.

As soon as the meeting was over, Lisa pulled her back the moment she was about to walk out the room and whispered, "We need to talk."

Playing dumb she smiled and asked, "What about?"

"Like the fact you sat through most of the meeting like you were zoned out. It's a good thing Mr. McCray didn't notice."

Jayla sobered quickly as she came to her senses. Having erotic flashbacks on her time was one thing, but having them on her employer's time was another. "Sorry."

Lisa laughed. "Hey, girlfriend, don't apologize. I'd trade places with you in a heartbeat. You've been with Storm Westmoreland again haven't you?"

Wondering how Lisa could know such a thing, Jayla asked innocently, "What makes you think that?"

Lisa raised a dark brow. "It's either that or you're reliving some dynamite memories. My guess is that you're reminiscing about the past twenty-four hours."

Jayla sighed as she closed the door so that she and Lisa could have total privacy. She sat back down at the table and Lisa joined her. She met her best friend's curious gaze. "Storm dropped by last night."

Lisa leaned back in her chair and grinned. "That's a first. I heard that once an affair was ended, Storm Westmoreland never looked back. Booty calls are not exactly his style."

Jayla shot her a frown and Lisa held up her hand apologetically. "Sorry. I was just making an observation."

Jayla let out a breath. That was one observation she didn't need. "He wants to take me out tomorrow night. To dinner. At Anthony's."

Lisa smiled. "Real classy place, so what's the problem?"

Jayla returned the smile. Lisa could be so good for her at times. "The problem is what you indicated earlier. Storm is not a man who looks up women from his past. I knew that in New Orleans and he knew that, and it was understood that when we returned to Atlanta we would have no reason to seek the other out."

Lisa nodded. "And he's seeking you out."

"Yes, and I can't let it happen."

Lisa sat up and leaned in closer. "Is it okay for me to ask why?"

Jayla dragged a hand through her hair, and drew in a frustrating breath. "Because it's lousy timing. My life is about to undergo some major changes, Lisa, for Pete's sake. My physical is set for next Friday and soon after that, I plan to get inseminated. The last thing I need is Storm deciding, for whatever reason, that I'm a novelty to him."

"Hey, Jayla, don't sell yourself short. There might be another reason that Storm Westmoreland finds you interesting, other than you being a novelty. The guy might actually like you. I mean really, really *like* you. There's a chance that you've blown him away."

Lisa's comments gave Jayla pause. She thought about that possibility all of two seconds and shook her head. "Impossible. Even if there was a remote chance that was true, Storm and I could never get serious about each other."

Lisa lifted a brow. "Why?"

Jayla frowned. "He's too much like my father. He would want to keep a tight rein on me. He actually believes a woman should be a stay-at-home mom. I guess he thinks the ideal woman is one he can keep barefoot and pregnant."

Lisa smiled. "Hey, I could do barefoot and pregnant with a man like him," she said, wiggling her eyebrows.

"Well, I can't. I have my life mapped out just the way I want, thank you. I'm having a baby without the complications of a man. The last thing I need is someone dictating how I should live my life and there's no doubt in my mind that Storm would be very domineering."

Lisa's smile widened. "Yeah, but also very sexy."

Jayla raised her gaze to the ceiling. "But I can't think of sexy when all I can see is domineering."

Lisa laughed. "Evidently you could last night if those blushes were any indication. But if you feel that way, you should let him know. It should be simple enough to tell him you aren't interested and to stop coming around."

Jayla nodded. Yes, that should be simple enough and she would tell him tomorrow night at dinner.

Storm walked into Coleman's Florist Shop and glanced at the older woman who was standing behind the counter. Luanne Coleman was considered one of the town's biggest gossips, but he still enjoyed doing business with her. And besides, none of the women he ever ordered flowers for lived in College Park, the suburb of Atlanta where he and the majority of his family resided and where his brother Dare was sheriff.

"Good morning, Ms. Luanne."

She glanced up from looking at the small television screen that was sitting on the counter. Her soaps were on. "Oh, hello, Storm. You want to send the usual?"

He smiled. By the usual, she meant a bouquet of fresh-cut flowers. "No, I want to send something different this time."

He knew that would grab her attention. She stared at him

for a long moment, then raised her brow over curious eyes and asked, "Something different?"

"Yes."

She nodded. "All right, what do you have in mind?"

He glanced around. "What do you have that will last a while?"

"I have plenty of live plants and they make beautiful gifts."

Storm nodded. He didn't recall seeing a live plant in Jayla's home and thought one would be perfect, especially in her bedroom for her to look at and remember. "Good. I want you to pick out the biggest and prettiest one, and this is the person I want it delivered to," he said, handing her a slip of paper.

She took it and glanced at the name. She then looked at him and smiled. "How much do you want to spend?"

A huge grin touched his lips. "The cost isn't important. Just add it to my account. And make sure it's delivered this afternoon."

She nodded and smiled as she quickly began writing up his order. "She must be very special."

Storm sighed heavily. There. He had heard someone else say what he'd been thinking all day, so the only thing he could do was smile and agree. "Yes, she is."

Jayla blinked at the man holding the huge potted plant in front of him. The plant was almost larger than he was. "Are you sure you're at the right address, sir?"

"Yes, I'm positive," the older man said, peeping from behind the bunch of healthy green leaves of a beautiful and lush looking areca palm. "It's for you."

Jayla nodded as she stepped aside to let the man bring

the plant inside, wondering who on earth could have sent it. When the man had placed it down, he turned to leave. "Wait, I need to give you a—"

"The tip's been taken care of," the man said. And then he was gone.

Jayla quickly pulled the card from the plant and read it.

> *Whenever you look at this, think of me.*
> *Storm*

Jayla's heart skipped a beat. No it skipped two, possibly three. She blinked, then sank down on her sofa. Storm had sent her a plant, a beautiful, large, lush green plant and for the first time in a long time, she was at a loss for words.

Nine

"Thanks again for the plant, Storm. It's simply beautiful."

"You're welcome and I'm glad you like it."

"And thanks for bringing me here, tonight. Everything was wonderful."

"You're welcome again."

Then she glanced around Anthony's, the stunning and elegant antebellum mansion that had a reputation of fine service and delicious food. Being here reminded her of New Orleans, and she wondered if perhaps that was the reason Storm had chosen this place.

She glanced back over at Storm and their gazes met. He'd been watching her, something she noticed he'd been doing all evening. He had arrived at her house promptly at seven and since she'd been ready, she had only invited him inside long enough for her to grab her purse and a wrap.

At least, that's what she had assumed.

The moment he had stepped inside her home, he had pulled her into his arms and kissed her, making her realize that although she wished otherwise, there was definitely something going on between them, something that had not ended in New Orleans.

She regarded him with interest and although she knew that she should broach the subject of why they were here, she wasn't ready to do that yet. Tonight was too beautiful to bring up any unpleasantries just yet. "So, how are things going at work?" she asked, after taking another sip of her wine.

In New Orleans, he had told her that he had made the transition from lieutenant to captain rather well, but hadn't gone into much detail. Because her father had been a fire captain for years, she was familiar with all the position entailed. She was well aware that today firefighters needed more training to operate increasingly sophisticated equipment and to deal safely with the greater hazards that were associated with fighting fires in larger, more elaborate structures, as well as wild fires.

In her eyes, all firefighters were heroes, but she knew being a fire captain also required strong leadership qualities. A captain had to possess the ability to establish and maintain discipline and efficiency, as well as direct the activities of the firefighters in his company.

"Work is fine, and how are things at Sala Industries?" he asked rousing her from her musings.

She smiled. "Things are great. In addition to working with Tara on the Kids' World charity benefit, I'm working on another project that involves an environmental agency."

He nodded. "And what about that project you were excited about? How is it going?"

She swallowed, knowing exactly what project he was

referring to. She worked her bottom lip between her teeth several times before responding. "I haven't started it yet."

She decided it was time to discuss the reason they were there. They had dodged the subject long enough. She met his eyes and a shiver ran through her when she saw the desire in their dark depths. Wanting to make love with him seemed natural. Too natural. It was a good thing they were in a public place.

Her body continued to stir and an unbearable heat spread through her. Trying to ignore her torment, she considered him for a long moment, then spoke, her voice barely above a whisper. "You said you would explain things tonight, Storm."

I did say that didn't I? Storm thought as his gaze continued to hold Jayla's. The only problem was that he wasn't any closer to answers today than he had been yesterday. The only thing that he was certain of was that he wanted to continue to see Jayla. He enjoyed being with her, taking her out and having fun with her and wanted to continue to do all those things they had done together in New Orleans. For some reason, she had his number and he was helpless to do anything about it.

"Storm?"

He blinked and realized while he'd been thinking that he had been staring at her like some dimwit. He cleared his throat. "Jayla, is there a possibility for us to start seeing each other?"

It was evident from the look on her face that his question surprised her. "Why?" she asked, regarding him as if the question were totally illogical.

"I like you."

She blinked, then threw him a grin that caught him off guard. "Storm, you like women. I know that much from your reputation."

He didn't like hearing her say that. They weren't talking about other women; they were talking about her. He didn't place her in the same category with those other women he'd dated before. To him, none of them could be compared to Jayla.

He watched as she leaned over the table and, with a curious arch of her brow, whispered, "It's the virginity thing, isn't it?"

Storm nearly stopped breathing. He blinked, not understanding just what she was asking him. Seconds later, it dawned on him just what she'd insinuated and he frowned. "Why would you think something like that?"

She straightened back in her chair and shrugged. "What else could it be? I was your first virgin. You said so yourself. So I'm a novelty to you." She picked up her wine glass to take another sip, smiled, then said, "Trust me, you'll get over it."

His frown deepened. "Tell me something," he said, leaning back in his chair. "When did you figure that out?"

Her smile widened. "What? That I'm a novelty to you or that you'll get over it?"

"That you're a novelty to me."

She licked her lips and Storm felt his gut catch. "The night you showed up at my place. Seeking me out was so unlike how you're known to operate, so I figured there had to be a reason, since any woman can basically please a man in bed. It slowly dawned on me why I was different."

Storm inhaled deeply. He was glad they were sitting at a table in the rear of the restaurant in an area where they were practically alone. He would hate for anyone to over-hear their conversation.

He shook his head slowly. Everything she'd said had sounded logical. With one exception. It was so far from the truth that it was pitiful.

He smiled. "First of all, contrary to what you think, Jayla, any woman cannot please a man in bed. When making love to a woman, most men…and women for that matter, experience various degrees of pleasure. On a scale from one to five, with five being the highest, most men will experience at least a three. In some situations, possibly a four, and only if they're extremely lucky, a five."

She lifted a brow. "How did I rate?"

Storm's smile widened. He'd known the curiosity in Jayla would give her the nerve to ask. In fact, he'd hoped that she would. "You rated a ten."

She blinked, then a smile touched the corners of her lips. "A ten?"

He chuckled. "Oh, yes, a ten."

He watched as she thought about it for a second, then she shook her head, perplexed and confused. "But—but how is that possible if a ten isn't on the chart?"

He reached across the table and captured her hand in his. "Because you, Jayla Cole, were off the charts." He watched her smile widen, evidently pleased with herself. Then he added, "And it had nothing to do with you being a virgin, but had everything to do with the fact that you are a very passionate woman."

He tilted his head and said, "It also had a lot to do with the fact that the two of us are good together. We click. When we make love, I feel a connection with you that I've never felt with another woman." What he didn't add was that when he made love to her, he felt as if they were made for each other.

"Wow, that's deep, Storm," she said regarding him seriously.

He sighed as he nodded. "Yeah, it is deep and that's why I'd like for us to continue to see each other."

Jayla inhaled. She would like to continue to see him, too, but she knew that wouldn't be a wise thing to do. In less than a month, she would be getting inseminated and hopefully soon after that, she would become pregnant. The last thing she needed was to get involved with anyone, especially Storm, no matter how tempting the thought was.

"Jayla?"

She met his gaze. "I don't think that would be a good idea, Storm. This new project will take up a lot of my time, and I won't have time for a relationship."

He considered her words. He was still curious as to what kind of project she would be working on. He had asked her about it in New Orleans and she had danced around an answer. The only thing he could come up with was that it involved her job, perhaps a confidential, top-secret assignment. "And there's no way we can work around this project?"

"No."

Her response had been quick. Definite. "When will you start?"

She shrugged. She would have her physical next Friday and then hopefully within three weeks after that, she would go in to have the procedure done. "Possibly within a month."

He met her gaze levelly. "Is there any reason we can't continue to see each other until then?" Slowly, he raised her hand to his lips and kissed it.

Jayla swallowed and knew what she should say. She should tell him yes, there were plenty of reasons why they couldn't continue to see each other for the next month, but for some reason she couldn't get the words out. What Storm had said earlier was true. They were good together. They clicked and they connected. And deep down, a part of her felt she needed this time with him. Afterwards, at least she would have her memories of their time together.

"No, there's no reason," she finally said. "But you will have to promise me something, Storm."

He kissed her hand again before asking. "What?"

"When I say it's over, then it's over. You won't drop by and you won't call."

He shook his head. "I can't agree to that, Jayla. I promised your father that I would periodically check on you and—"

"I'm not talking about that, Storm. I'm taking about you dropping by or calling with the intention of us becoming involved again. You have to promise me when I say it's over, that it will be over. No questions asked."

Storm stared at her for a long moment as emotions tumbled inside of him. They were feelings he didn't understand, but he knew that no matter what, things would never be over between them, project or no project. He would see to it.

"All right," he agreed. "You'll be calling the shots and I'll abide by your wishes."

"Hey, Storm, are you in this game or not?"

Storm glanced over at Thorn and frowned. "Yes, I'm in."

"Well, keep your mind on the game. You're daydreaming again."

Storm's frown deepened. "Yeah, whatever." He glanced across the table at his four brothers who had smirks on their faces. "What's so funny?"

It was the oldest brother, Dare, who answered. "Word's out on the streets that some woman has finally caught the eye of the Storm. I pulled old man Johnson over the other day for running a Stop sign, and he said that he'd heard you were so besotted with some gal that you can't pee straight."

When Storm narrowed his eyes, Dare held up his hand. "Hey, those were Mr. Johnson's words, not mine."

Chase chuckled. "And I've heard that you're sending so many flowers to this woman that the money Coleman Florist is making off you is the reason Mrs. Luanne has that new swing on her front porch."

"And I heard," Stone piped in, as a huge smile touched his lips, "that you've been seen all over Atlanta with her and that she's a beauty. Funny that we haven't met her yet."

Thorn added, "Hey, Storm, what happened to your 'love them and leave them' policy?"

Storm leaned back in his chair thinking that Thorn's question was a good one, but one he didn't intend to answer.

"I've seen her," Chase said grinning. "She came into the restaurant one day to have lunch with Tara."

"Tara?" Thorn asked, raising a curious brow. "Tara knows her?"

Chase nodded. "Evidently, since they had lunch together that day. However, I don't know if Tara knows that Storm has the hots for her."

"Excuse me, guys," Storm said interrupting his brothers' conversation. "I don't appreciate you discussing my business like I'm not here."

Stone chuckled. "All right, then we'll discuss your business like you're here." He then looked at Chase. "So, is she as good-looking as everyone claims she is?"

Chase grinned. "Yeah. She's Adam's daughter all grown up."

Thorn frowned. "Adam? Adam Cole, Storm's boss who died a few months back?"

"Yep."

Stone glanced over at Storm. A curious glint shone in his eyes. "You're actually seeing Adam Cole's girl?"

Angrily, Storm stood and threw down his cards. "That's it. I'm out of the game."

Dare stared up at his youngest brother. Being the oldest, he had to occasionally bring about peace…and in some situations, order. "Sit back down, Storm, you're getting overheated for nothing. And to be quite honest with you, for all intents and purposes, you've been out of the game since you got here. You haven't been concentrating worth a damn all night."

One of Dare's dark eyebrows lifted. "And what's wrong with us wanting to know about this woman that you're seeing? As your brothers, don't you think we have a right to at least be curious?"

Storm inhaled deeply as he glanced around the table and glared. "I don't appreciate any of you discussing her as if she's like the other women I've dated."

Dare nodded. "If she's not like the other women you've dated, then it's up to you to tell us that. There's nothing wrong with letting us know that you think she's special, instead of trying to keep her a secret," he said in a low voice.

Storm sat back down and glanced around at his brothers. They were staring at him, waiting expectantly. He sighed deeply. "Her name is Jayla Cole and yes, she's Adam's daughter all grown up and we're seeing each other. We're taking things slow, one day at a time, and yes, she's special. Very special."

Stone smiled. "When will we meet her?"

Storm leaned back in his chair. "I'll introduce her to everyone the night of the charity benefit for Kids' World. Her company is a corporate sponsor and she's working closely with Tara to pull things together for that night."

Dare nodded. "And all of us will look forward to meeting her then." He glanced around the table and grinned. "Now let's play cards."

Jayla sat curled up on her sofa and glanced around her living room, thinking the past week had been like a scene from a romance novel. Storm had sent her flowers practically every single day and had wined and dined her to her heart's content.

On Saturday night, they had gone to a laser show on Stone Mountain and then on Sunday evening, he had taken her to a movie. Because he had been at the station all day Monday, she didn't see him again until Tuesday night, when he'd dropped by with Chinese food. They had sat eating at her kitchen table while she had told him about how her day had gone and how things were coming together for this weekend's charity benefit.

They had talked about his day, as well. He had told her that he had been selected to head up the city's fire prevention program for the coming year and that he was excited about that.

She glanced down at the letter she had in her hand, the same letter that had arrived last week from the fertility clinic reminding her of tomorrow's appointment. Seeing it and rereading it had reaffirmed her decision to have the procedure.

She nearly jumped when she heard the phone ring. Thinking that perhaps it was Storm, she placed the letter on the table, then quickly moved across the room to answer it. He had called earlier and said he would be playing cards tonight with his brothers rather late and that he would see her tomorrow. "Yes?" she said, after picking up the phone.

"It's Lisa. How are things going?"

Jayla smiled. Lisa had been out of town most of the week on business. "Everything's going fine. How was your trip?"

"Wonderful. I love Chicago. You know that."

Jayla chuckled. Yes, she did know that. Lisa enjoyed shopping and Chicago was her favorite place to shop.

"So, are you planning to keep your appointment tomorrow?"

Lisa's question immediately silenced Jayla's thoughts. She frowned. "Of course, why wouldn't I?"

"Because from what you told me every time I've called this week, you and Storm have been seeing a lot of each other."

Jayla shrugged. "So? What Storm and I are sharing is short-term. I know that and so does he."

"But it doesn't have to be that way, Jayla. I believe things could last if you gave them a chance."

Jayla rolled her eyes to the ceiling. "Lisa, trust me, they won't. What Storm and I share is physical. I'm enjoying his company and he's enjoying mine. Why does it have to be more than that?"

For a long moment, there was silence. Then Lisa asked softly, "What are you afraid of, Jayla?"

Jayla flinched. "I'm not afraid of anything."

"I think that you are. Storm Westmoreland is everything a woman could want in a man and you are in a good position to be that woman. Why are you willing to turn your back on such a wonderful opportunity?"

Jayla closed her eyes. She could never be the kind of woman Storm wanted. Besides, he wasn't what she wanted, either. At the moment, no man was. She wanted a baby and not a complicated relationship. She'd long ago given up on finding Mr. Right. The "married with children" routine was a fairy tale that might never come true for her. Her biological clock was ticking and she had made the decision to start a family sooner rather than later.

She turned when she heard a knock at the door. "Look Lisa, there's someone at the door. I'll talk with you later. Bye."

After hanging up the phone, she glanced at the clock on the wall, then crossed the living room to the door. It was late, after midnight. The only reason she was still up was because she had taken the morning off for her physical at the fertility clinic. Since her appointment wasn't until nine, that meant she would get to sleep late.

She knew before she got within a foot of the door that her late-night visitor was Storm. That would explain the reason her heart was beating so fast and her senses were getting heated. She tried forcing her conversation with Lisa out of her mind. Her best friend was wrong and she wasn't afraid of anything, especially a serious relationship with Storm. She merely chose not to have one.

"Who is it?"

"Storm."

She quickly opened the door and he stood there, staring at her. His eyes were dark, intense, and she immediately recognized the look in them. Her lips curved into a smile. "Hi."

He returned her smile and the heat infiltrating her senses kicked up another notch. "Hi, yourself. The card game ended and I wasn't ready to go home."

"Oh?"

"I had to see you, Jayla."

A teasing glint shone in Jayla's eyes. "Okay, you see me. So now what?"

He slowly took a couple of steps forward, and she took a couple of steps back. When he was completely inside the house, he closed the door behind him and locked it. He walked the few feet over to her, cupped her shoulders in his hands and pulled her to him, her mouth just inches from his. "Now this," he breathed against her lips.

Then kissed her.

As soon as their mouths touched, Storm felt something hot rush through his bloodstream. The scent of Jayla, as well as the taste of her, was getting to him and the only thing he could think of doing was devouring her, making love to her. Suddenly, some emotion that he'd never felt before flared within him, almost bringing him to his knees, and he finally acknowledged it for what it was.

Love. He loved her.

Storm drew back and stared at her for a quick second before his mouth came back down on hers again. His hands were everywhere as he began removing her clothes, and broke off the kiss just long enough to remove his own. Then he swept her into his arms and carried her into the bedroom.

What should have been a no-brainer had been hard as hell for a staunch bachelor like him to figure out. The reason he had wanted a relationship with Jayla had nothing to do with them being great together in bed, but everything to do with emotions he hadn't been able to recognize until tonight.

He was in love with Jayla Cole. She had caught more than the eye of the Storm. She had captured his heart.

Ten

Anchoring himself above Jayla on his elbows, Storm looked down at her and smiled. Dang, she always looked beautiful after experiencing an orgasm. What more could a man ask for than to be right there to experience each one with her.

He sighed deeply. Now that he knew he loved her, he had to figure out a way to get her to fall in love with him as well. First, he would have to gain her complete trust, and then he had to make sure she clearly understood that he was her Mr. Right and wanted a long-term relationship with her, one that ended in marriage. A smile curved his lips. Yeah, that's what he wanted, Jayla as his wife.

"Why are you smiling?"

He met her gaze. Her eyelids were heavy and her cheeks had a sated flush. Leaning down, he brushed a kiss across her lips. "After what we've just shared, how can you ask me that?"

As usual, everything had been perfect. The way their bodies had come together while a trail of fire had blazed between them. It was a fire he hadn't wanted to put out, but instead had done everything within his power to ignite even further, to make it burn out of control.

And it had.

By the time he had entered, she had been delirious with desire, begging breathlessly for him to make love to her; she'd been a she-cat, clawing his back and nipping his shoulders. And when they had finally come together, she had cried out his name and he had continued to move inside of her, taking them to heights of profound pleasure.

He loved her, he thought in wonder, as he leaned down and murmured her name against her cheek. "Mind if I stay the night?"

He felt her smile against his lips. "Umm, I would be highly disappointed if you didn't," she said softly.

He chuckled. "In that case, I'll stay." He pressed his mouth to hers and kissed her, needing the taste of her again. Moments later, he slowly pulled back and flicked his gaze over her features. Heat immediately surged through his groin. If he didn't get out bed, he would be making love to her all over again, and she needed her rest.

"I'll turn off the lights," he whispered.

"All right, but hurry back."

He grinned as he eased out of bed and slipped into his jeans. And just think he'd assumed that she needed her rest. He glanced at the huge plant that sat in the corner. It was just where he'd wanted it, in her bedroom so she could think of him whenever she saw it.

As he walked out of the bedroom, the image of Jayla's sexy smile when she'd told him to hurry back filled his mind and made him want to do just as she'd requested. When he got to the living room, he leaned down to turn off the lamp near the sofa and his gaze caught sight of a letter lying on the coffee table. It was a letter from a fertility clinic.

Without thinking that he didn't have any right to do so, he picked up the letter and read it. A few seconds later, he sank down on her sofa, not believing what he had just read. He felt stunned. Confused. Jayla had sought out the services of a fertility clinic to get artificially inseminated with some stranger's sperm? Why?

He reread the letter, thinking there must be a mistake but again the contents were the same. She was scheduled to have a physical tomorrow—which actually was today— and then, when it was determined her body would be most fertile, she would go in to have the procedure done.

"You were supposed to hurry back."

Storm stood when Jayla walked out of the bedroom. When she saw the letter in his hand, she quickly crossed the room and snatched it from him. "You had no right to read that, Storm."

He just stared at her as every muscle in his body vibrated. Confusion gave way to anger. "Then how about you telling me what this is all about."

She glared at him. "It's private and personal and doesn't concern you."

"Doesn't concern me? Like hell, it doesn't. If it concerns you, then it concerns me. Are you actually considering having your body inseminated with some man's sperm?"

Jayla tipped her head back; her anger clashed with his. He'd made it sound as if what she planned to do was something filthy and degrading. "It's not what I'm considering doing, it's what I will be doing. I made the decision months ago."

Taken back by Jayla's statement, he wiped a hand down his face as if doing so would erase his anger. When he looked over at her, she was standing with her hands on her hips, glaring at him. A thought suddenly popped into his head. "Wait a minute. Is this the project you've been so excited about lately?"

"Yes."

He shook his head, not believing the conversation they were having. "I understand the need for that procedure in certain situations, but not with you. Why would you even consider doing such a thing, Jayla?"

Her eyes were consumed with fire. "Because I want a baby that's why! I want a baby more than anything."

Storm was shocked by that revelation. She had once mentioned she wanted to have kids, but she had never given him the idea that she'd been obsessed with having one. "And you want a child to the point where you would actually consider having a baby from someone you don't know?"

"Yes. In fact, I prefer it that way. I want a baby and not the baby's father. I don't want a man coming in my life trying to run things."

"Run things how?"

"Like telling me how to live my life, forcing the issue of whether I can have a career outside of my home, a man who'd try to control me and keep a tight rein on me."

Of all those things she'd named, Storm recognized only one that he might eventually become guilty of.

"And what's wrong with a man wanting the sole responsibility of taking care of his wife so she won't have to work outside the home?"

Her glare thickened. "For some women, nothing, but I prefer taking care of myself. I don't want to depend on anyone."

Storm frowned and crossed his arms over his chest. "So, for your own selfish reasons, you're willing to deny your child a father?"

"If it means not wasting my time looking for a Mr. Right who doesn't exist, then yes."

Storm tried to keep his anger in check. Why couldn't she see that he was her Mr. Right? He slowly shook his head again. "If you want a baby, then I'll give you *my* baby."

"What!"

"You heard me. I'll be damned if I'll let another man get the woman I love pregnant."

Jayla was shocked at the words he'd spoken. "The woman you love?"

Silence shredded the air and Storm knew he had to get her to understand the depth of how he felt. He crossed the room and with his fingertip, lifted her chin to meet his gaze. "Yes. I love you, Jayla, and if you want a baby, then we'll get married and I'll give you one."

She stared at him as if she didn't believe he'd suggested such a thing. And then she took a step back from him. "Things wouldn't work between us, Storm. You would want more from a wife than I'm willing to give."

"And what about the fact that I love you?"

She shrugged. "I believe you like sleeping with me, but I find it hard to believe that you really love me, Storm."

She sighed deeply when he didn't say anything but continued to stare at her. "We agreed that we would end things between us whenever I was ready," she finally said to break the silence. "Well, I'm ready. For us to continue seeing each other will only complicate matters."

"Complicate matters like hell!" he said, his voice rising. "I tell you that I love you and that I want to marry you and give you the baby you want, and you're telling me that you don't believe a word of it and to get out of your life? And to top things off, you plan to continue with this crazy scheme to have a baby from a man who not only doesn't love you, but a man *you* don't even know?"

"I don't owe you an explanation for anything I do, Storm. And considering everything, it would be best if you left."

Storm stared at her for a moment, then moved past her to the bedroom. Moments later, fully dressed, he came back into the living room. He stood in front of her and said softly, "I hope that one day you'll take your blinders off. Maybe then you'll recognize your Mr. Right when he comes and stands right in front of you."

He then turned and walked out the door.

When Storm left, Jayla moved around the house trying to convince herself that she was glad they would no longer be seeing each other. The last thing she needed was a man trying to control her life.

After closing things up and turning off the lights, she slipped back into bed, and tried to ignore the scent of Storm that still lingered there. She closed her eyes.

I love you, Jayla...

She opened her eyes, flipped on her back and stared up at the ceiling as she tried to convince herself that she wasn't the one with blinders on, he was. Couldn't he see that what he was feeling wasn't really love but lust? Die-hard bachelors like Storm didn't fall in love in a blink of an eye or after a few rolls between the sheets.

She turned to her side and closed her eyes, trying to

force thoughts of Storm from her mind. But she couldn't. Steeling herself, she sighed, knowing the memories of the times they'd spent together were too deep, too ingrained in her memory.

Getting over him wouldn't be easy, but dammit she would try. She would shift her focus elsewhere and appreciate the good things that were happening to her. Everything she'd wanted was falling in place. Tomorrow, she would go to the fertility clinic for her physical and then she would wait eagerly for the day when she would be inseminated.

Storm was not the most important thing to her—having a baby was.

"Hey, Captain, you got a minute?"

Storm glanced up from the stack of papers on his desk. After having a sleepless night, he had gotten up at the crack of dawn to come into the station. Most of his men hadn't arrived yet. Although it wasn't a requirement, he was one of those captains who preferred working the same hours as the firefighters he supervised.

"Sure, Cobb, come on in. What can I do for you?"

Darryl Cobb had recently become a father again. Four months ago, his wife Haley had given birth to their third child. Darryl was a few years younger than Storm and they had known each other since their high school days. He'd also known Darryl's wife, Haley, from high school, as well, and remembered Darryl and Haley dating even back then. Evidently, Haley hadn't had a problem recognizing Darryl as her Mr. Right since the two of them had been married for over ten years now and always seemed happy together.

"I was wondering if I can take a few hours off today. The

baby has a doctor's appointment and Haley just called. Her boss called an important meeting for later today."

Storm nodded. Haley was a computer programmer for a financial management company. "That shouldn't be a problem," Storm said, turning to check the activity board. "You're supposed to teach a class on fire prevention at that elementary school today. Do you have a replacement?"

Darryl smiled. "Sure do. Reed has agreed to cover for me."

Storm nodded. The one thing he liked about the men he supervised was that they got along and were quick to help each other out when something unexpected came up. "In that case, your taking a few hours off won't be a problem," he said making a notation on the activity sheet.

He glanced back over at Cobb. "So how has it been going since Haley returned to work?"

Darryl chuckled. "Crazy."

"Then why did she go back?" he asked, then quickly felt he'd been out of line for asking such a question. But from the laugh Cobb gave him, evidently he hadn't been surprised by the question. From Storm's early days as a fire-fighter, it had been a joke around the station that his views on women working inside the home were unrealistic and so outdated they were pitiful. He'd been told that it would be hard as hell to find a woman who'd agree to do nothing but stay at home, barefoot and pregnant.

"Well, that humongous house we just bought in Stone Mountain was one good reason for her to return to work," Darryl said, still chuckling. "But another reason is that Haley enjoys what she does and I'm not going to ask her to give it up." He looked pointedly at Storm and said, "That's where a lot of men make their mistakes."

Storm raised a brow. "Where?"

Darryl smiled. "In assuming that they are the only ones who have it together. I personally think it's women who really have it together, and we're merely bystanders looking in. Besides, with Haley and me both sharing equally in the raising of our kids, I feel I'm playing just as an important role in their lives as she is, and that's important to me. It has nothing to do with which one of us is bringing home the bacon, but mainly how the both of us are serving the bacon. Together, we're forming a deep, nurturing attachment to our children and are giving them all the love we have, which is a lot. And to me that's the most important thing."

A few moments later after Cobb had left, Storm stood at the window in his office and looked out as he thought about what Darryl had said. Was one of the reasons Jayla hadn't recognized him as her Mr. Right was because in her mind he was all wrong?

Had what Nicole done to him all those years ago driven his beliefs that a husband should be sole provider for his wife and family? He would be the first to admit that because of Nicole's rejection, he'd always wanted to prove the point that a man, highly educated or not, could take care of his household. His father had done it and had raised a family on a construction worker's salary.

He thought of his brothers and their wives. Even married to a sheikh, his sister Delaney was still working as a pediatrician and doing one hell of a job raising their son Ari, who was beginning to be a handful. But then her husband Jamal also played an equally important role in raising their son. Then there were his sisters-in-laws, Shelly, Tara and Madison. Although Shelly and Dare were the only ones who had a son, eleven-year-old AJ, Storm was fairly certain that if Tara and Madison were to get pregnant, they wouldn't consider giving up their careers.

He closed his eyes and remembered the scene that had played out in Jayla's living room last night. The woman he loved was planning to let another man get her pregnant only because she was convinced there wasn't a Mr. Right for her. She actually believed there wasn't a man who could and would understand her need to be in control of her life.

He opened his eyes and glanced down at his watch. According to that letter he'd read last night, she had a physical at nine this morning at that fertility clinic. After the physical, it would probably be two to three weeks before the actual procedure could be performed. Hopefully that would give him time to convince Jayla that he really did love her, and that he would satisfy all her needs, including her need to remain independent…to a certain degree. Changing his conventional views wouldn't be something he could do overnight, but it was something he could definitely work on, especially for Jayla.

The most important thing was to show her that he was the right man for her. The only man for her. For the second time since returning from New Orleans, the old fortune teller's words crept into his thoughts.

You should keep your sights high, be patient and let destiny take its course.

He smiled. Perhaps the old woman hadn't been a flake after all and had known exactly what she'd been talking about. Tomorrow was the night of the charity benefit and because of her involvement, he knew Jayla would be there. He would start wooing her with the intensity of a man who had one single goal in his mind.

To win the love of the woman he intended to marry.

* * *

"You can go ahead and get dressed, Ms. Cole," the nurse said smiling. "The doctor will return in a few minutes to go over the results of your tests."

"Thanks."

Jayla sighed deeply as she began putting her clothes back on. She'd had a sleepless night and hadn't been as excited about the appointment this morning as much as she'd wanted to be because of thoughts of Storm. And it hadn't helped matters that she'd been crying most of the morning.

She walked over to the mirror in the room and looked at herself. She looked pathetic. Her reflection revealed a woman who was truly drowning in her own misery. And it was a misery well deserved. Even Lisa hadn't given her any slack when she'd called this morning and she'd told her about the argument she'd had with Storm. And when she'd mentioned that Storm had told her that he loved her and wanted to marry her, her best friend had actually gone off on her. But then, what was a best friend for if she couldn't give you hell when you needed it?

The sad thing about it was that everything both Storm and Lisa had said was true. She wouldn't recognize her Mr. Right if he came to stand right in front of her.

She sighed deeply as she slipped back into her panty hose. So what if Storm was one of those men who wanted to take care of his woman? Wasn't it better to have a man who wanted to take care of you than to have a man who expected you to take care of him? And was it so awful that he was a little on the conventional side? She would be the first to admit that she found some of his old-fashioned ways sweet. Besides, if his conventional way of thinking became too much for her, couldn't she just make it her business to modernize him? And so what if he had ways like her father? Adam Cole had been a great parent and a part of her could now say she appreciated her strict upbringing. A couple of the girls she had wanted to hang around with in high school had either gotten pregnant before graduating or had gotten mixed up with drugs.

Upon waking this morning, it had taken several hours of wallowing in self-pity, as well as being forced to listen to Lisa's tirade, before she'd finally taken the blinders off. Storm loved her and he was her Mr. Right and she loved him. She couldn't fight it, nor could she deny the truth any longer. She loved him and had always loved him.

Oh, she understood now why he had kept his distance so many years ago but still, it had been a bitter pill for a young girl to swallow. A part of her had built up an immunity against ever being rejected by him again. But now she was a woman and she wanted what any other woman would want—a man to love her. And that man had offered to marry her and give her the baby she wanted. How blessed could a woman be?

Her feeling of euphoria quickly disintegrated when she remembered she had thrown his words of love back in his face. She had a feeling that Storm was a man who wouldn't take rejection well. What if he never wanted to see her again?

She quickly slipped into her skirt, thinking she had to work fast to correct the mistake she'd made or she would lose him completely. And the first thing she had to do was to cancel her plans to get inseminated. The only man she wanted to father her child was Storm.

She turned when she heard a knock at the door. "Come in." She smiled apologetically when Dr. Susan Millstone walked in. Before the doctor could say anything she quickly said, "I've changed my mind."

After closing the door behind her, Dr. Millstone tilted her head and looked at her. "You've changed your mind?"

"Yes. I've decided not to go through with the artificial insemination procedure after all."

The doctor leaned against the closed door. "May I ask the reason you've changed your mind?"

Jayla smiled. "Yes. The man that I love wants to marry me and give me his child, and I want that, too, more than anything." *And I hope and pray I haven't lost him*, she thought.

Dr. Millstone chuckled as she shook her head. "What you've just said will make what I have to tell you a little easier."

Jayla raised a brow. "Oh?"

"I just went over the results of your physical and it seems you're already pregnant."

The news was so shocking that Jayla dropped into a nearby chair. She looked back up at the doctor, not believing what she'd been told. "I'm pregnant?"

The doctor chuckled again. "Yes. You're almost a month along."

Jayla shook her head, as if trying to keep it from spinning. She was almost a month pregnant! "New Orleans," she said softly, as a smile touched her lips.

"Excuse me?"

She met Dr. Millstone's grin. "I said New Orleans. I got pregnant in New Orleans. But how is that possible when we were careful?"

A smiled played at the corner of Dr. Millstone's mouth. "I deliver a lot of babies whose parents thought they were careful, too. No birth control is one hundred percent."

Jayla chuckled. "Evidently not."

"So, can I assume that you're happy with the news?"

Jayla jumped up as the feeling of euphoria took control of her again. "Yes, I'm happy! I am ecstatic!" she said, laughing joyously. She just hoped and prayed that Storm would be happy and ecstatic, as well, when she told him that she loved him and was having his baby.

Eleven

Everyone who was somebody in Atlanta had turned out for the Kids' World charity benefit. There were politicians, CEOs of major corporations, celebrities and well-known sports figures, all of whom considered Atlanta home.

There was also a sheikh in attendance, the very handsome Prince Jamal Ari Yasir, who was dressed in his native Middle Eastern attire and causing quite a stir among the ladies, single or otherwise. Jayla smiled, knowing the stir was a waste of time and effort since it was well known that Prince Yasir was happily married to the former Delaney Westmoreland, Storm's sister.

Jayla glanced across the room at the group of men standing together laughing and talking. Although Storm hadn't arrived yet, it didn't take much to recognize the men as Westmorelands. Their kinship was clearly evident in their facial features, their height as well as their sex appeal.

She began wondering if perhaps Storm had changed his mind about coming. After leaving the clinic yesterday, she had decided to take the rest of the day off. Too excited to work, she had gone home and called Lisa and invited her to lunch.

She'd barely gotten the words out after Lisa arrived when she burst into tears of happiness. Then she told Lisa of her fears about telling Storm. What if he no longer loved her? What if her rejection had killed his feelings for her?

Lisa, in her usual optimistic way, had assured her that although Storm might be a little angry with her right now, she doubted his love could have died so quickly.

Jayla had wanted to call and ask him to come over, but then she'd remembered he was on duty at the fire station. So, instead of talking to him yesterday, she had walked around the house wondering what she would say when she saw him tonight.

"Everything looks beautiful, doesn't it?"

Jayla turned when she recognized the voice of Tara Westmoreland. Tara was accompanied by three other women whom Jayla didn't immediately recognize. At first, Jayla thought each of the women was beautiful in a unique way. Like Tara, they were smiling and each of their smiles reflected a sincere friendliness. Jayla returned their smiles as Tara made the introductions.

The women were Shelly Westmoreland, who was married to Sheriff Dare Westmoreland; Madison Westmoreland, who was married to Stone Westmoreland and Storm's sister, Delaney Westmoreland Yasir. Jayla swallowed deeply. All three women, like Tara, were part of the Westmoreland clan. Somehow, Jayla found her voice to respond to Tara's earlier comment. "Yes, everything is beautiful and your committee should be proud of what they've accomplished."

Tara chuckled. "Yes, but your company also played a huge role. The food is wonderful. Everyone is talking about the catering service that is being used. It's quite evident that Sala Industries went out of their way tonight."

"Thanks."

"And I have to say the dress you're wearing looks simply gorgeous on you," the woman who had been introduced as Madison Westmoreland said.

"Thank you," Jayla said smiling, beginning to feel more relaxed.

She and the women launched into a discussion of styles in clothing and movies they'd recently seen when they heard a sudden buzzing from a group of single women standing not far away. A quick glance at the entrance to the ballroom revealed why. Storm and his cousin Ian had walked in and were crossing the ballroom floor to join the other Westmoreland men. Both men looked dashing and handsome dressed in black tuxedos.

Part of Jayla wished Storm would look her way; then, seconds later, she decided maybe it would be best if he didn't when she overheard the conversation between two women standing not far away.

"Hey, I'm going to make it my business to go after 'The Perfect Storm' tonight," the more statuesque of the two said.

The other women giggled and said. "Storm Westmoreland has a reputation of not doing the same woman twice."

"Yeah, but I heard that just once is all it takes to blow your mind and I definitely intend to have that one time," the statuesque one countered.

A flash of jealousy raced through Jayla, and she started

to turn to the woman and tell her that when it came to Storm, hands off. But she couldn't do that. She didn't have the right.

She glanced up when she felt someone gently touch her arm. "I wouldn't worry about what the 'hottie duo' are saying if I were you," Shelly Westmoreland whispered, smiling. "I heard from a very reliable source that Storm has found a special lady and only has eyes for her."

Jayla blinked in surprise at Shelly's words and glanced at the other women standing beside her. They all nodded; evidently, they'd heard the same thing. Was it possible that they knew she and Storm had been seeing each other? And who was this reliable source Shelly Westmoreland was talking about? Had Storm mentioned her to members of his family?

Her heart stopped and she wasn't sure what to say to the four women who were staring at her with such genuine and sincere smiles on their faces. Tears pressed at the corner of her eyes.

"I may have lost him," she whispered, as her mind was suddenly filled with doubt and regret.

Delaney Yasir chuckled and placed an arm around Jayla's shoulder. "I doubt that. My brother hasn't taken his eyes off of you since he arrived."

Hope ran through Jayla. "Really?" She was standing with her back to Storm so she couldn't see him.

Madison Westmoreland grinned. "Yes, really."

"Hey, Storm, you want something to drink?" Jared Westmoreland asked his cousin as he grabbed a glass a wine off the tray of a passing waiter.

"Storm doesn't want anything to drink," Ian said, grinning. "The only thing Storm wants is that woman who's standing over there talking to the Westmoreland women."

Stone Westmoreland lifted a brow and glanced across the room. The woman's back was to them, so he couldn't get a look at her. "You've met her?" he asked in surprise.

Ian chuckled. "Yes, Storm introduced us in New Orleans."

That comment got everyone's attention. Chase stared at Storm. "You took her to New Orleans with you?"

Before Storm could respond, not that he would have anyway, Ian spoke up. "Of course he didn't take her to New Orleans with him," he said, as if the thought of Storm taking any woman out of town with him were ludicrous. "They just happened to be in the same place at the same time. Her father was Storm's old boss, Adam Cole."

Thorn Westmoreland took a slow sip of his drink and said, "Her parentage is old news, Ian, but her being in New Orleans with Storm is definitely something that we didn't know about."

"And something all of you are going to forget you heard," Storm said. The tone of his voice matched the look on his face. Highly irritated. Totally annoyed. Deadly serious. "And I thought I told you guys that I don't like you discussing my business like I'm not here."

Chase gave his twin a dismissive shrug and said, "Yeah, whatever." He then turned his attention back to Ian. "So what else can you tell us about Storm's lady?"

Ian met Storm's gaze and got the message loud and clear, although it was obvious his brothers hadn't…or they chose no to. Ian grinned and decided to play dumb. "I forget."

Storm smiled. He knew he could count on Ian to keep his secrets, just as Ian knew he could count on him to keep his. Things had always been that way between them. He then turned his attention back to Jayla and wished the crowd would thin out so his view wasn't as blocked, or that she would at least turn around so he could see her. He wanted to look into her eyes to let her know that no matter how much she might want him out of her life, he was there to stay.

Moments later, as if he had willed it to be so, the crowd thinned out and she turned and met his gaze. His heart almost stopped when he saw how radiant she looked. And what made her even more beautiful was the fact that she was wearing that red dress.

His dress.

It was the same one he had picked out for her in New Orleans. He wondered, hoped and prayed that there was a hidden meaning behind her wearing that dress. Could he dare hope she might realize that he was her Mr. Right? Knowing there was only one way to find out, he walked away from the group.

His destination was the woman he loved.

Jayla's breath caught in her throat when she saw Storm heading toward her. She couldn't tell from his expression whether he was glad to see her or not, but one thing was certain—he wasn't going to avoid her. But maybe she was jumping to conclusions. Although he was headed to where she was standing, he might be coming over to say hello to his sister and sisters-in-law since they were standing next to her.

"Here comes Storm Westmoreland," she overheard one of the women from the "hottie duo" say. "And I think he's seen my interest and is coming over to talk to me."

"Fat chance of that happening," Tara whispered. Jayla couldn't help but smile and hoped Tara was right. As Storm got closer, her hope went up a notch when she saw he was still holding her gaze. She sighed deeply when he stopped in front of her.

"Hi, Jayla."

She smiled up at him and tried to keep her heart from pounding erratically in her chest. "Hi, Storm."

It was only then that he released her gaze and glanced at his sister and sisters-in-law. "Good evening, ladies, and, as usual, all of you look beautiful and bestow much pride upon the Westmoreland name."

He glanced back at Jayla. "And you look beautiful, as well, Jayla."

"Thanks." And before she lost her nerve, she asked, "Is there a chance I might speak with you privately for a moment?" The man standing before her looked so irresistibly handsome, so utterly gorgeous that it almost took her breath away.

Her pulse quickened when he stared into her eyes with an intensity that made her shiver. He nodded, then said, "Sure." He shifted his gaze from her to the others and said, "Please excuse us for a minute." After taking her hand in his, Storm led her through the doors and outside into the lobby.

"There're a lot of people here tonight," Storm said, as they continued walking down the elegant and immaculate hallway.

"Yes, there are," Jayla replied. The benefit was being held in the ballroom of the Atlanta Civic Center and the facility was the perfect place to host such an event. She wondered where Storm was taking her. It was obvious that wherever it was, he wanted them to have privacy.

They stopped walking when they came to a beautiful

atrium. All the greenery, flowering plants and the huge waterfall added warmth and even more grace and style to their surroundings. Jayla suddenly felt nervous, not sure of herself, but then she knew she had to say her piece. No matter what, he deserved to know about their baby, but she couldn't tell him that now. If he wanted her back, it had to be because he still loved her and not because he would feel obligated because she was carrying his child.

She cleared her throat. "Storm."

"Jayla."

She smiled when they had spoken at the same time. She glanced at him and his features were expressionless and she had no idea what he was thinking.

"Ladies first," he said, meeting her gaze.

Jayla swallowed. She knew that a lot was at stake here, but she remembered the words her father would often say—*nothing ventured, nothing gained*. She cleared her throat. "I kept my appointment at the clinic this morning."

He contemplated her silently for a moment, and then asked, "Did you?"

She expelled a soft breath, still unable to read him. "Yes, but I've decided not to go through with the procedure." She thought she saw relief flash through his gaze but wasn't sure.

He held her gaze steadily, studied her for a moment. "Why did you change your mind?" he asked.

Jayla swallowed again as she lifted her chin. "Because I realized that you were right and that I did have blinders on. So I took them off and when I did, I could see things a lot clearer."

Tension hummed between them; she felt it. "And what do you see, Jayla?" he asked softly.

She breathed deeply and decided to tell him just what she saw. "I see a tall man who is so strikingly handsome I can barely think straight, who has eyes so dark they remind me of chocolate chips and a voice so sexy it sends shivers down my spine. But most importantly, since taking my blinders off, I can see my Mr. Right standing right in front of me. Now. At this very minute. And I pray that I haven't ruined things, and there's a possibility that he still wants me, because, since taking off my blinders, I've also discovered just how much I love him and just how much I want him in my life."

Jayla held her breath, not knowing what he would say, not knowing if he would accept her words. Then, she saw a slow smile come into his face and spread from corner to corner on his lips. And those lips leaned down and came mere inches from hers and whispered. "I'm glad you quickly came to that conclusion, Jayla Cole, because I love you and there was no way in hell I intended to let you go."

Before she could say anything, he captured her mouth in a kiss. It was a kiss that was so powerful and tender that it immediately brought tears to her eyes. Storm loved her and she loved him and she believed in her heart that everything would be okay. Together, they would make their marriage work because love was the main ingredient and she believed they had plenty of that.

He reluctantly broke off their kiss. "I know you can't leave until everything is over, but I have to get you alone."

Jayla grinned and glanced around. "We're alone now, Storm."

He chuckled. "Yeah, but this place is too public for what I want to do to you." His features then turned serious. "But more importantly, Jayla, we need to talk and come to an understanding about a few things, all right?"

She nodded. "All right. But no matter what, we'll work things out."

He pulled her back into his arms. "Most definitely."

It was well after midnight when Jayla entered Storm's home. The evening had been perfect and a lot of money had been raised for Kids' World, which meant that plenty of terminally ill children's dreams would be coming true. It wasn't hard to guess that the calendars would sell like hotcakes. Over one hundred thousand calendars had been sold, and an order had already been placed for that many more.

And it hadn't come as a surprise to anyone that the single women had gone wild over the twelve men who had posed for the calendar, especially Mr. July, Thorn Westmoreland. However, any women who might have given thought to the possibility that she had a chance with Mr. July, married or not, discovered just how wrong they were when, after receiving the plaque that had been presented to all twelve men, Thorn crossed the room and kissed his wife, proclaiming to all that Tara Westmoreland was all the woman he wanted and needed.

And, Jayla thought as she inwardly smiled, Storm had made a number of declarations himself tonight. That single woman who'd vowed that she would get at least one time with Storm had been brazen enough to approach him while he and Jayla had stood together talking. Storm had smoothly introduced Jayla to the woman as his fiancée. The woman had congratulated them and walked off, thoroughly disappointed.

He had also introduced her to his parents and the rest of his family. She even got to meet the newest additions to the Westmoreland clan, his cousins Clinton, Cole and

Casey. She had quickly decided that the Westmoreland family was a very special one and they all stuck together like glue.

"Would you like something to drink, Jayla?"

She turned and watched as Storm closed the door and locked it. "No, thanks." She nervously glanced around and stopped when her gaze came to rest on a framed photograph that sat on his fireplace mantle. It was a photo that the two of them had taken with her father at his last birthday party, the one the men at the fire station had given him. Her father had insisted that she and Storm stand next to each other while he stood in the background. Because of Adam Cole's six-seven height, he appeared to be towering over them. And he was smiling so brightly that she couldn't help wondering if perhaps he'd known about her feelings for Storm and, in his own special way, had given them his blessings that night, because less than five months after that picture was taken, he'd died.

Storm followed her gaze and after a few moments said, "Whenever I look at that picture and really study it, I think that your father was a lot smarter than either of us gave him credit for being."

Jayla nodded. Evidently their thoughts had been on the same page. She inhaled deeply and then met Storm's gaze. "I agree." She broke eye contact with him and continued her study of his home. With earth-toned colors and basic furnishings, it was clearly a bachelor's place. But everything was neat and in order. "Nice place."

"Thanks. A few months ago, I decided to sell it and get a bigger place," he said as his gaze roamed over her from head to toe. "Thanks for wearing that dress. It's my favorite."

Jayla smiled. "That's the reason I wore it. I was trying to give you a sign, or at least make you remember the time we spent together in New Orleans. I figured the only other person who would know I'd worn this dress before was Ian, and I counted on him not noticing."

Storm lifted a brow. He hated to tell her, but Ian had noticed. In fact, every man who'd been present tonight had noticed Jayla Cole in *that* dress. And each and every time he saw a man looking at her, even when trying not to, he was inwardly overjoyed that she belonged to him.

And now with her standing in the middle of his living room, there was nothing he was itching to do more than to take that dress off her because chances were, like before, the only thing underneath that dress was a pair of thongs. But he knew before they could get to the bedroom, there were issues that needed to be resolved between them.

Sighing, he slowly crossed the distance that separated them and took her hand in his. "Come on, let's sit down and talk."

She nodded and then he led her over to the leather sofa and they sat down. "I've done a lot of thinking, Jayla, and you're right. There's nothing wrong with a woman working outside the home if she wants to do so. The reason I was opposed to it was because years ago, while a senior in high school, I thought I was in love with a girl who threw my love back in my face when I told her of my decision not to go to college but to attend the Firefighters Academy instead. She said that a man without a college education could not properly take care of the needs of his family. When she said that, something snapped inside me and I intended to prove her wrong and, with college or not, I wanted to be a man who could sufficiently provide for all of my family's needs."

Jayla nodded. She could see the pride of a man like Storm getting bruised with a woman saying something like that. She sighed, knowing it was time to get rid of her emotional baggage as well.

"Because Dad was so strict on me while I was growing up," she started off by saying, "I had this thing against marrying a man who I thought would try and control me. But now I see that Dad had the right approach in raising me, or no telling how I might have turned out."

She inhaled in a deep breath, then added, "I believe all those times I thought I was looking for Mr. Right I failed miserably because it wasn't time to find my Mr. Right. It wasn't time until I saw you again in New Orleans."

Storm lowered his mouth to hers and the kiss he gave her was filled with so much intensity and passion, Jayla couldn't help the groan that purred from her throat. Nor could she ignore the sudden rush of heat that threatened to consume her entire body as Storm continued to claim her mouth, staking a possession all the way to the darkest recesses of her soul. She kissed him back, putting into the kiss all the love and feeling that he did, claiming his mouth as well and staking her possession.

He pulled back, stood and pulled her into his arms. "Will you marry me, Jayla Cole? Will you love me for better or worse, richer or poorer, in sickness and in health, till death do us part?"

Tears gathered in Jayla's eyes. "Yes! Oh, yes! I love you."

Storm grinned. "And I love you, too." His gazed locked with hers and smiled. "Tell me again what you see."

She smiled up at him, knowing it was time to tell him her other news. "I see my Mr. Right…and," she whispered softly, "I also see the man who is the father of my baby."

Jayla watched Storm's expression and knew the exact moment it dawned on him what she'd said. For a moment,

he continued to gaze at her, his dark eyes clouded with un-
certainty, hope. "Did you just say what I think you said?"
he asked breathlessly.

She smiled. If there was any doubt in her mind that he
wanted a baby, their baby, it evaporated when she saw the
look of sheer happiness in his eyes. "Yes. After taking my
physical, I told the doctor that I had changed my mind
about the insemination procedure and she said it was a
good thing since I was already pregnant."

Jayla chuckled. "By my calculations, I got pregnant in
New Orleans but I still can't figure out how that happened
when I know for certain that protection was used every
time we made love."

Storm laughed. "Yeah, but a condom can only hold
so much, sweetheart. When a man is driven to have
multiple—"

Jayla placed a finger to Stone's lips and grinned. "Okay,
I get the picture."

He swept her into his arms and chuckled. "I'm glad that
you do and I guess you know what your pregnancy means,"
he said as he moved toward his bedroom.

"What?"

"There's no way we'll have a June wedding, even if you
wanted one. We're getting married as soon as possible."

She laughed. "How soon?"

"Tomorrow isn't soon enough for me."

"What about in a month?"

"Umm, that's negotiable," he said as he placed her in
the middle of his bed.

When he stood back, Jayla's gaze swept over him. When
she saw the magnitude of his arousal, she inhaled deeply. "I
have a feeling I might not be able to move in the morning."

He smiled as he began removing his clothes. "I have a feeling you just might be right. And I have a feeling that if you weren't pregnant now, you would very well be in the morning."

Jayla smiled and her gaze met his. "And you're sure you're okay with becoming a father, Storm? It's a lot for a devout bachelor to take on a wife and child at the same time."

His smile widened. "But I won't have a ordinary wife and child," he said coming back to her, completely naked. "They will be extraordinary because they are mine. And I promise to take very good care of them, Adam's daughter and grandchild, just as I believe he knew that I would."

He leaned over and slowly peeled the dress from Jayla's body. Then he quickly removed her shoes and panty hose. Finally, he removed her thong. "I really like that dress, but I like you naked a lot better."

He then joined her on the bed. "Do you know what is about to happen to you, Jayla?"

She laid a hand against his cheek. "No, tell me," she implored softly, seeing the dark, heated look of desire in his eyes. It was a look that sent sensuous shivers all through her body.

He smiled. "You're about to be taken by *Storm*."

Jayla smiled. She was definitely looking forward to that experience.

Epilogue

A month later

"You may kiss your bride."

As the Westmoreland family looked on in the backyard of his parents' home, Storm smiled as he turned to Jayla and captured her mouth in the kind of a kiss that everyone thought should have been saved for later, but one he was determined to bestow upon his bride anyway.

"At least he has his own woman to kiss now," Dare whispered to Thorn.

"It's about damn time," Thorn Westmoreland replied, grinning.

Finally, Storm tore his mouth away from Jayla and smiled. He then leaned over and whispered something in her ear and whatever he said made her blush profusely.

"Umm, I wonder what he said that made her blush like that, considering the fact she's already pregnant," Stone whispered to Chase.

Chase shrugged. "You know Storm. Nothing about him surprises me."

"Well, hell, I'm still in shock," Jared Westmoreland said, shaking his head. "Storm was the last Westmoreland I thought would marry, and just think in less than nine months he'll be a daddy."

Jared then chuckled as he glanced at Dare, Thorn, Chase and Stone. "What is it with your side of the family? All of you are tying the knot."

Chase frowned. "Not all of us."

Stone smiled. "Your time is coming, Chase." He then glanced over at his cousins, Ian, Jared, Spencer, Durango, Quade, Reggie, Clint and Cole. "And all of yours."

Durango narrowed his eyes. "Don't try putting a damn curse on us like that old woman put on Storm."

Dare shook his head laughing. "She didn't put a curse on Storm, she merely read his palm. Besides, if it's going to happen, then it's going to happen. The big question is who's next."

He studied his remaining single brother and his eight male cousins. He smiled, having an idea just who the next Westmoreland groom would be, and he couldn't wait to see it happen.

He grinned. "All I have to say is that when it happens, don't fight it. You'll find out later that it will be the best thing to ever happen to you."

Quade Westmoreland frowned. "No disrespect, Sheriff, but go to hell." He turned and walked off, and the other single Westmoreland men did likewise.

Dare laughed and he kept on laughing while thinking there would definitely be another Westmoreland wedding before long. He would bet on it…if he were a betting man.

* * * * *

Silhouette® Desire®

introduces an exciting new family saga with

DYNASTIES: THE DANFORTHS

A family of prominence... tested by scandal, sustained by passion!

THE CINDERELLA SCANDAL by Barbara McCauley
(Silhouette Desire #1555, available January 2004)

MAN BENEATH THE UNIFORM by Maureen Child
(Silhouette Desire #1561, available February 2004)

SIN CITY WEDDING by Katherine Garbera
(Silhouette Desire #1567, available March 2004)

SCANDAL BETWEEN THE SHEETS by Brenda Jackson
(Silhouette Desire #1573, available April 2004)

THE BOSS MAN'S FORTUNE by Kathryn Jensen
(Silhouette Desire #1579, available May 2004)

CHALLENGED BY THE SHEIKH by Kristi Gold
(Silhouette Desire #1585, available June 2004)

COWBOY CRESCENDO by Cathleen Galitz
(Silhouette Desire #1591, available July 2004)

STEAMY SAVANNAH NIGHTS by Sheri WhiteFeather
(Silhouette Desire #1597, available August 2004)

THE ENEMY'S DAUGHTER by Anne Marie Winston
(Silhouette Desire #1603, available September 2004)

LAWS OF PASSION by Linda Conrad
(Silhouette Desire #1609, available October 2004)

TERMS OF SURRENDER by Shirley Rogers
(Silhouette Desire #1615, available November 2004)

SHOCKING THE SENATOR by Leanne Banks
(Silhouette Desire #1621, available December 2004)

Available at your favorite retail outlet.

If you enjoyed what you just read,
then we've got an offer you can't resist!

Take 2 bestselling love stories FREE!

Plus get a FREE surprise gift!

Clip this page and mail it to Silhouette Reader Service™

IN U.S.A.
3010 Walden Ave.
P.O. Box 1867
Buffalo, N.Y. 14240-1867

IN CANADA
P.O. Box 609
Fort Erie, Ontario
L2A 5X3

YES! Please send me 2 free Silhouette Desire® novels and my free surprise gift. After receiving them, if I don't wish to receive anymore, I can return the shipping statement marked cancel. If I don't cancel, I will receive 6 brand-new novels every month, before they're available in stores! In the U.S.A., bill me at the bargain price of $3.80 plus 25¢ shipping and handling per book and applicable sales tax, if any*. In Canada, bill me at the bargain price of $4.47 plus 25¢ shipping and handling per book and applicable taxes**. That's the complete price and a savings of at least 10% off the cover prices—what a great deal! I understand that accepting the 2 free books and gift places me under no obligation ever to buy any books. I can always return a shipment and cancel at any time. Even if I never buy another book from Silhouette, the 2 free books and gift are mine to keep forever.

225 SDN DZ9F
326 SDN DZ9G

Name	(PLEASE PRINT)	
Address	Apt.#	
City	State/Prov.	Zip/Postal Code

Not valid to current Silhouette Desire® subscribers.

Want to try two free books from another series?
Call 1-800-873-8635 or visit www.morefreebooks.com.

* Terms and prices subject to change without notice. Sales tax applicable in N.Y.
** Canadian residents will be charged applicable provincial taxes and GST.
  All orders subject to approval. Offer limited to one per household.
  ® are registered trademarks owned and used by the trademark owner and or its licensee.

DES04R

©2004 Harlequin Enterprises Limited

COMING NEXT MONTH

#1627 ENTANGLED—Eileen Wilks
Dynasties: The Ashtons
Years ago, Cole Ashton and Dixie McCord's passionate affair had ended when Cole's struggling business had taken priority over Dixie. Now, she was back in his life and Cole hoped for a second chance. But even if he could win Dixie once more, would Cole be able to make the right choice this time?

#1628 HER PASSIONATE PLAN B—Dixie Browning
Divas Who Dish
Spunky nurse Daisy Hunter never thought she'd find the man of her dreams while on the job! But when a patient's relative, athlete Kell McGee, arrived in town, she suddenly had to make a difficult decision—stick to her old agenda for finding a man or switch to passionate Plan B!

#1629 THE FIERCE AND TENDER SHEIKH—Alexandra Sellers
Sons of the Desert
Sheikh Sharif found long-lost Princess Shakira fifteen years after she'd escaped her family's assassination. As the beautiful princess helped heal her homeland, Sharif passionately worked on mending Shakira's spirit. Though years as a refugee had left her hardened, could the fierce and tender sheikh provide the heat needed to melt Shakira's cool facade and expose her heart?

#1630 BETWEEN MIDNIGHT AND MORNING—Cindy Gerard
When veterinarian Alison Samuels moved into middle-of-nowhere Montana, she hardly expected to start a fiery affair, especially with hunky young rancher John Tyler. To J.T., this tantalizing older woman was a stimulating challenge and Alison was more than game. But J.T. hid a dark past and Alison wasn't one for surprises....

#1631 IN FORBIDDEN TERRITORY—Shawna Delacorte
Playboy Tyler Farrel was totally taken when he laid eyes on the breathtakingly beautiful Angie Coleman. She was all grown up! Despite their mutual attraction, Ty wouldn't risk seducing his best friend's kid sister until Angie, sick of being overprotected, decided to step into forbidden territory.

#1632 BUSINESS AFFAIRS—Shirley Rogers
When Jenn Cardon placed the highest bid at a bachelor auction, she had no idea she'd just landed a romantic getaway with sexy blue-eyed CEO Alex Dunnigan—her boss! Thanks to cozy quarters, sexual tension turned into unbridled passion. Alex wasn't into commitment but Jenn had a secret that could keep him around...forever.

SDCNM1204

SAGA

USA TODAY bestselling author

JOAN ELLIOTT PICKART

brings you a brand-new story in her
bestselling MacAllister family saga…

MacAllister's Return

When Assistant D.A. Jesse Burke
finds out that he was stolen as a
baby, he heads to California to
discover his true heritage—and
finds unexpected love with
TV news anchor Krista Kelly.

"Joan Elliott Pickart gives a delightful read via
inviting characters and a soft and light style."
—*Romantic Times*

Coming in January 2005.

Where love comes alive™

**Exclusive
Bonus Features:**

**Author Interview
Sneak Preview…
and more!**